Madame Zero

by the same author

HAWESWATER
THE ELECTRIC MICHELANGELO
THE CARHULLAN ARMY
HOW TO PAINT A DEAD MAN
THE BEAUTIFUL INDIFFERENCE
THE WOLF BORDER

as co-editor

SEX AND DEATH

MADAME ZERO

· Stories ·

SARAH HALL

First published in 2017
by Faber & Faber Limited
Bloomsbury House
74–77 Great Russell Street
London WC1B 3DA

Typeset by Faber & Faber Limited
Printed in the UK by CPI Group (UK) Ltd, Croydon, CR0 4YY

A CIP record for this book
is available from the British Library

ISBN 978-0-571-29001-7

2 4 6 8 10 9 7 5 3 1

For L and L

The more clearly one sees this world, the more one is obliged to pretend it does not exist.

JAMES SALTER

· Contents ·

· Mrs Fox ·

That he loves his wife is unquestionable. All day at work he looks forward to seeing her. On the train home, he reads, glancing up at the stations of commuter towns, land-steal under construction, slabs of mineral-looking earth, and pluming clouds. He imagines her robe falling as she steps across the bedroom. Usually he arrives first, while she drives back from her office. He pours a drink and reclines on the sofa. When the front door opens he rouses. He tries to wait, for her to come and find him, and tell him about her day, but he hasn't the patience. She is in the kitchen, taking her coat off, unfastening her shoes. Her form, her essence, a scent of corrupted rose.

Hello, darling, she says.

The shape of her eyes, almost Persian, though she is English. Her waist and hips in the blue skirt; he watches her move – to the sink, to the table, to the chair where she sits, slowly, with a woman's grace. Under the hollow of her throat, below the collar of her blouse, is a dribble of fine gold, a chain, on which hangs her wedding ring.

Hello, you.

He bends to kiss her, his hands in his pockets. Such simple pleasure; she is his to kiss. He, or she, cooks; this is the modern world, both of them are capable, both busy. They eat dinner, sometimes they drink wine. They talk or listen to music; nothing in particular. There are no children yet.

Later, they move upstairs and prepare for bed. He washes his face, urinates. He likes to leave the day on his body. He wears nothing to sleep in; neither does his wife, but she has showered, her hair is damp, darkened to wheat. Her skin is incredibly soft; there is no corrugation on her rump. Her pubic hair is harsh when it dries; it crackles against his palm, contrasts strangely with what's inside. A mystery he wants to solve every night. There are positions they favour, that feel and make them appear unusual to each other. The trick is to remain slightly detached. The trick is to be able to bite, to speak in a voice not your own. Afterwards, she goes to the bathroom, attends to herself, and comes back to bed. His sleep is blissful, dreamless.

Of course, this is not the truth. No man is entirely contented. He has stray erotic thoughts, and irritations. She is slow to pay bills. She is messy in the bathroom; he picks up bundles of wet towels every day. Occasionally, he uses pornography, if he is away for work. He fantasizes about other women, some of whom look like old girlfriends, some like his wife. If a woman at work or on the train arouses him, he wonders about the alternative, a replacement. But in the wake of these moments, he suffers vertiginous fear, imagines losing her, and he understands what she means. It is its absence which defines the importance of a thing.

And what of this wife? She is in part unknowable, as all clever women are. The marrow is adaptable, which is not to say she is guileful, just that she will survive. Only once has she been unfaithful. She is desirable, but to elicit adoration there must be more than sexual qualities. Something in her childhood has made her withheld. She makes no romantic claims, does not require reassurance, and he adores her because of the lack. The one who loves less is always loved more. After she has cleaned herself and joined him in bed, she dreams subterranean dreams, of forests, dark corridors and burrows, roots and earth. In her purse, alongside the makeup and money, is a small purple ball. A useless item, but she keeps it – who can say why? She is called Sophia.

Their house is modern, in a town in the corona of the city. Its colours are arable: brassica, taupe, flax. True angles, long surfaces, invisible, soft-closing drawers. The mortgage is large. They have invested in bricks, in the concept of home. A cleaner comes on Thursdays. There are similar houses nearby, newly built along the edgelands, in the lesser countryside – what was once heath.

One morning he wakes to find his wife vomiting into the toilet. She is kneeling, retching, but nothing is coming up. She is holding the bowl. As she leans forward the notches in her spine rise against the flesh of her back. Her protruding bones, the wide-open mouth, a clicking sound in her gullet: the scene is disconcerting, his wife is almost never ill. He touches her shoulder.

Are you all right? Can I do anything?

She turns. Her eyes are bright, the brightness of fever. There is a coppery gleam under her skin. She shakes her head. Whatever is rising in her has passed. She closes the lid, flushes, and stands. She leans over the sink and drinks from the tap, not sips, but long sucks of water. She dries her mouth on a towel.

I'm fine.

She lays a hand, briefly, on his chest, then moves past him into the bedroom. She begins to dress, zips up her skirt, fits her heels into the backs of her shoes.

I won't have breakfast. I'll get something later. See you tonight.

She kisses him goodbye. Her breath is slightly sour. He hears the front door slam and the car engine start. His wife has a strong constitution. She does not often take to her bed. In the year they met she had some kind of mass removed, through an opened abdomen; she got up and walked the hospital corridors the same day. He goes into the kitchen and cooks an egg. Then he too leaves for work.

Later, he will wonder, and through the day he worries. But that evening, when they return to the house, will herald only good things. She seems well again, radiant even, having signed a new contract at work for the sale of a block of satellite offices. The greenish hue to her skin is gone. Her hair is undone and all about her shoulders. She pulls him forward by his tie.

Thank you for being so sweet this morning.

They kiss. He feels relief, but over what he's not sure. He untucks her blouse, slips his fingers under the waistband of her skirt. She indicates her willingness. They move upstairs and reduce each other to nakedness. He bends before her. A wide badge of hair, undepilated, spreads at the top of her thighs. The taste reminds him of a river. They take longer than usual. He is strung between immense climactic pleasure and delay. She does not come, but she is ardent; finally he cannot hold back.

They eat late – cereal in bed – spilling milk from the edges of the bowls, like children. They laugh at the small domestic adventure; it's as if they have just met.

Tomorrow is the weekend, when time becomes luxurious. But his wife does not sleep late, as she usually would. When he wakes she is already up, in the bathroom. There is the sound of running water, and under its flow another sound, the low cry of someone expressing injury, a burn, or a cut, a cry like a bird, but wider of throat. Once, twice, he hears it. Is she sick again? He knocks on the door.

Sophia?

She doesn't answer. She is a private woman; this is her business. Perhaps she is fighting a flu. He goes to the kitchen to make coffee. Soon she joins him. She has bathed and dressed but does not look well. Her face is pinched, dark around the eye sockets, markedly so, as if an overnight gauntening has taken place.

Oh, poor you, he says. What would you like to do today? We could stay here and take it easy, if you don't feel well.

Walk, she says. I'd like some air.

He makes toast for her but she takes only a bite or two. He notices that the last chewed mouthful has been put back on her plate, a damp little brown pile. She keeps looking towards the window.

Would you like to go for a walk now? he asks.

She nods and stands. At the back door she pulls on leather boots, a coat, a yellow scarf, and moves restlessly while he finds his jacket. They walk through the cul de sac, ringed by calluna houses, past the children's play area at the end of the road, the concrete pit with conical mounds where children skate. It is still early; no one is around. Intimations of frost under north-facing gables. Behind the morning mist, a faint October sun has begun its industry. They walk through a gateway onto scrubland, then into diminutive trees, young ash, recently planted around the skirt of the older woods. Two miles away, on the other side of the heath, towards the city, bulldozers are levelling the earth, extending the road system.

Sophia walks quickly on the dirt path, perhaps trying to walk away the virus, the malaise, whatever it is that's upsetting her system. The path rises and falls, chicanes permissively. There are ferns and grasses, twigs angling up, leaf-spoils, the brittle memory of wild garlic and summer flowers. Towards the centre, a few older trees have survived; their branches heavy, their bark flaking, trunks starred with orange lichen. Birds dip and dart between bushes. The light breaks through; a gilded light, terrestrial but somehow holy.

She moves ahead. They do not speak, but it is not uncompanionable. He allows himself, for a few moments, to be troubled by irrational thoughts – she has a rapid, senseless cancer and will waste, there will be unconscionable pain, he will hold a fatal vigil beside her bed. Outliving her will be dire. Her memory will be like a wound in him. But, as he watches her stride in front, he can see that she is fit and healthy.

Her body swings, full of energy. What is it then? An unhappiness? A confliction? He dares not ask.

The woods begin to thicken: oak and beech. A jay flaps across the thicket, lands on the ground nearby; he admires the primary blue elbow before it flutters off. Sophia turns her head sharply in the direction of its flight. She picks up her pace and begins to walk strangely on the tips of her toes, her knees bent, her heels lifted. Then she leans forward and in a keen, awkward position begins to run. She runs hard. Her feet toss up fragments of turf and flares of leaves. Her hair gleams – the chromic sun renders it livid. She runs, at full tilt, as if pursued.

Hey, he calls. Hey! Stop! Where are you going?

Fifty yards away, she slows and stops. She crouches on the path as he hurries after her, her body twitching in an effort to remain still. He catches up.

What was all that about? Darling?

She turns her head and smiles. Something is wrong with her face. The bones have been re-carved. Her lips are thin and her nose is a dark blade. Teeth small and yellow. The lashes of her hazel eyes have thickened and her brows are drawn together, an expression he has never seen, a look that is almost craven. A trick of kiltering light on this English autumn morning. The deep cast of shadows from the canopy. He blinks. She turns to face the forest again. She is leaning forward, putting her hands down, lifting her bottom. She has stepped out of her laced boots and is walking away. Now she is running again, on all fours, lower to earth, sleeker, fleeter. She is running and becoming smaller, running and becoming smaller, running in the light of the reddening sun, the red of her hair and her coat falling, the red of her fur and her body loosening. Running. Holding behind her a sudden, brazen object, white-tipped. Her yellow scarf trails in the briar. All vestiges shed.

She stops, within calling distance, were he not struck dumb. She looks over her shoulder. Topaz eyes glinting. Scorched face. Vixen.

October light, no less duplicitous than any season's. Bird calls. Plants shrivelling. The moon, palely bent on the horizon, is setting. Everything, swift or slow, continues. He looks at the fox on the path in front of him. Any moment, his wife will walk between the bushes. She will crawl out of the wen of woven ferns. The undergrowth, which must surely have taken her, will yield her. How amazing, she'll whisper, pointing up the track.

These are his thoughts, standing in the morning sun, staring, and wrestling belief. Insects pass from stalk to stalk. The breeze through the trees is sibilant.

On the path, looking back at him, is a brilliant creature, which does not move, does not flinch or sidle off.

No. She turns fully and hoists the tail around beside her like a flaming sceptre. Slim limbs and slender nose. A badge of white from jaw to breast. Her head thrust low and forward, as if she is looking along the earth into the future. His mind's a shock of useless thought, denying, hectoring, until one lone voice proceeds through the chaos. You saw, you saw, you saw. He says half words, nothing sensible. And now she trots towards him down the path, as a dog would, returning to its master.

Nerve and instinct. Her thousand feral programmes. Should she not flee into the borders, kicking away the manmade world? She comes to him, her coy, sporting body held on elegant black-socked legs. A moment ago: Sophia. He stands still. His mind stops exchanging. At his feet, she sits, her tail rearing. Exceptional, winged ears. Eyes like the spectrum of her blended fur. He kneels, and with absolute tenderness, touches the ruff of her neck, which would be soft, were it not for the light tallowing of hairs.

What can be decided in a few moments that will not be questioned for a lifetime? He collects her coat from the nearby bushes. He moves to place it, gently, around her – she does not resist – and, his arms reaching cautiously under, he lifts her. The moderate weight of a mid-sized mammal. The scent of musk, gland, and faintly, faintly, her perfume – a dirty rose.

And still, in the woods and on the apron of grassland, no one is hiking, though soon there will be dogs tugging against leads, old couples, children gadding about. Down the path he walks, holding his fox. Her brightness escapes the coat at both ends; it is like trying to wrap fire. Her warmth against his chest is astonishing – for a wife who always felt the cold, in her hands and feet. She is calm; she does not struggle, and he bears her like a sacrifice, a forest Pietà.

Half a mile in secret view. Past the sapling ash trees, through the heath gate, past the concrete pit where one sole girl is turning tricks on her board, practising before the boys come, her gaze held down over the front wheels. There are the houses – new builds, each spanking, chimneyless, their garages closed – and he must walk the gauntlet of suburbia, his heart founding a terrible rhythm at the thought of doors opening, blinds being lifted, exposure. Somewhere nearby a car door slams. She shifts in his arms and his grip tightens. Around the bend; he ignores the distracted neighbour who is moving a bin. Up the pathway to number 34. She is heavier now, deadening his muscles. He moves her to the crux of his left arm, reaches into his trouser pocket for the keys, fumbles, drops them, bends down. She, thinking he is releasing her perhaps, begins to wriggle and scramble towards the ground, but he keeps her held in his aching arm, he lifts the keys from the flagstones, opens the door and enters. He closes the door behind and all the world is shut out.

Suddenly his rescuer's strength goes. His arms give. Sensing it, she jumps, her back claws raking his forearm. She lands sheerly on the carpet. She holds still a second or two, shakes, then goes into the kitchen, directly, no investigation of location, and jumps onto a chair next to the table. As if only now, after her walk and purging of the disease of being human, she is ready for breakfast.

These first hours with his new wife pass, not in wonderment, nor in confusion or fugue, but in a kind of acute discerning. She positions herself in the house, wherever she fancies, as she might otherwise have. He follows, making sure she has not vanished, making sure he is conscious. The spectacular evidence remains. He is able to approach. He is able to touch the back of her head, under the slim, almost bearded jaw, even the pads of her paws, which are so sensitive her flesh quivers. Like a curious lover he studies her form. The remarkable pelt, forged as if in a crucible of ruddy, igneous landscapes. The claws that have left long angry scratches on his arm: crescent-shaped, blond and black. The triangular, white-lined ears, with tall, dark guard hairs. The bend in her hind legs; the full, shapely thighs, similar, in a way, to a woman squatting. He studies sections, details. Her eyes, up close, are the colour of the Edwardian citrine brooch he bought her for her birthday.

He speaks quietly, says things she might want to hear, consolations. I am sorry. It will be all right. The day is lost. For much of it she sleeps. She sleeps curled on the floor. Her ribs palpitate. As dusk arrives he tries to eat, but can't. He picks her up and carries her to the bed. She repositions and closes her eyes again. Gently, he lies down next to her. He puts a hand to her side, where she is reddest. The texture of her belly is smooth and delicate, like scar tissue; small nubbed teats under the fur. Her smell is gamey; smoky, sexual.

Sophia, he whispers, don't worry, though she is not, as far as he can tell, distressed.

He closes his eyes. Sleep, the cure for all catastrophes, will bring relief, perhaps even reverse.

When he wakes there is the faint lunar bloom of streetlight in the bedroom and she is gone. He starts up. He moves through the house, desperately, like a man searching for a bomb. No dream could ever be so convincing. He rushes downstairs, and at the bottom treads in something slightly crusted and yielding. Quickly, he searches on. He calls out her name, feeling ever more its falseness.

She is standing on the kitchen table, an unmistakable silhouette, cut from the wild. She is looking out of the French windows at the garden, the nocturnal world. She is seeing what alien sights? The fresnel lenses of owl's eyes, luminous grassy trails, or bats blurting across the lawn? The grisly aroma of what he has trodden in rises to his nose. He wipes his foot on the carpet. He sits at the table and puts his head in his hands. She watches the garden.

Sunday. Monday. He fields phone calls from his and her places of work. He manages to lie convincingly, asks for personal leave. There is no milk. He drinks black tea. He eats cold soup, a stump of staling bread. He puts down bowls of water on the kitchen floor, but either she does not like the purity or the chlorine. He sits for hours, thinking, silent – every time he speaks he feels the stupidity of words. What has happened? Why? He is not able to unlock anything reasonable in his mind. She is in the house, a bright mass, a beautiful arch being, but he feels increasingly alone. He does not let her out, cruel as it seems, though she pays particular attention to the doors and vents where small draughts of outside air can be felt and smelled – he watches her sniffing the seal, gently clawing the frame. If this does not pass, he thinks, he will take himself to the doctor, or her to the veterinary – one of them will discover the truth, the contraspective madness. But then, how can he?

The sound of a key in the front-door lock startles him. He has been lying naked on the bedroom floor while she patrols. It is Esmé, the cleaner. It is Thursday. Nine a.m. He pulls on a robe, dashes down the stairs, and catches her just as she is coming into the hallway, dropping her bag on the floor, the door gaping open behind her.

No, he shouts. No! Go away. You have to go.

He puts a hand on her shoulder and begins to manoeuvre her backwards, towards the door. She gasps in shock at such treatment. Her employer is never home when she cleans – all she knows of him is the money he leaves on the table, the addressed letters she moves from doormat to counter, and it's his wife who speaks to her on the phone. She barely recognizes him, and for a moment mistakes him for an intruder.

What? What? Take your hands off. I, I'll –

She is alarmed, he can see, at the blockade, at being handled by a dishevelled, undressed man. He gathers his wits, releases her arm.

Don't clean this week, Esmé. We have a terrible bug. It's very contagious. I don't want to risk you getting it.

He is pale, a little crazed, but does not look ill.

Sophia has it?

Yes. She does.

Does she need anything? I can go to the pharmacy.

I'm taking care of her. Thank you. Please –

He gestures for her to leave. Routed, Esmé picks up her bag and steps away. He closes the door behind her, moves to the hall window and watches. She glances up at the bedroom, frowns, walks to her little blue car, gets in, and drives away. When he turns round the fox is standing at the top of the stairs.

Later that day, tense with anxiety, he leaves the house and goes to the library. He researches the world of madness. *Folie à deux.* Imposter delusion. Cotard. Capgras. Madame Zero. Mineness and the self's relations. But is it she or he who is lost? Then: Transmogrification. Fables. If he can avail himself of understanding, reason, definition . . . He returns home with medical texts and a slender yellow volume from the twenties. There is little correlation to myth. He is no thwarted lover. Most upsetting is the repetition of one aspect: an act of will.

So it continues. He enters a room and at first does not notice that she is up on top of the cabinet, on the windowsill, in the sliding food rack, which he has left open. Her poise so still she is entirely missable, the way all wild things are, until the rustic outline comes into focus. The surprise of seeing her, every time, in proximity; a thing from another realm that he has brought home. She sleeps. She sleeps neatly in a circle, tail tucked under her chin. Not on the bed, where he keeps trying to put her, but on a chair seat, in the corner of the utility room. The house is warm but she makes the most of extra heat wherever she can find it – the seat he has just vacated, or under the boiler. He cleans away the black, twisted scat that he finds, almost odourless now, tries not to be disgusted. If we were old, he tells himself, if I were her carer. He leaves plates of food on the floor, milk-soaked bread, cooked chicken, inoffensive dishes, which she investigates, tries, but does not finish. Instead she looks up at him, her brows steepling, haughty, unsatisfied. Part of his brain will not translate what she wants: that she must have it raw. Her eyes flicker after birds in the garden. Even trapped behind glass, she calculates. The metrics of the hunt.

Hating the humiliation, he brings home a can of dogfood, tips the jellied lump out onto a china dinner plate. She rejects it. He finds her licking her lips and trotting out of the kitchen. On the expensive slate floor is a dark patch of saliva – she has eaten something, a spider perhaps.

He cannot speak to her anymore. She doesn't understand and his voice sounds ridiculous to his own ears, a cacophony. She will not tolerate being in the same room for long. She roams, sniffs at the back door. She wants what's outside, she is becoming restive, growling, but he knows he cannot let her go. What would become of her, and, with her, his hope?

He inches around the front door when he leaves and locks it behind, is careful when re-entering the house. He phones and tells the cleaning woman her services are no longer needed.

And he knows; in this terrible arrangement, it is he who is not adjusting; he who is failing their relationship. So he decides. He buys uncooked meat from the butcher, offal, and in a moment of bravado, throws it onto the floor in front of her. She nips at a purple lobe, then walks away. Surely she is hungry! You are a fool, he tells himself. The next day he goes to a specialty shop and brings home a live bird. A pigeon. Its wings are clipped. He sets it on the floor, where it hops and tries to lift. Within moments she is beside it, crouching, lit with energy. He watches as she recoils and then pounces high, higher than she need, in excitement or prowess, and comes down hard on the helpless flurrying thing. She bites its iridescent neck. She twists its head. She is like machinery; the snapping and clicking of her teeth. The lavender breast is opened; there are riches inside. He turns and leaves, feeling sickened. He is angry and ashamed. That she could ever, even before this, be his pet.

It cannot go on – the proof is everywhere. Musk on the doorframes. Stains on the carpet. Downy feathers. And his unnatural longing, which can never be resolved, nor intimacy converted, even as his mind nudges against the possibility. Whatever godly or conjugal test this is, he has certainly failed. He decides. He opens the utility door and leaves it standing wide. He sits outside with his back against the cold house wall. In the garden is a muddy, mushroomy smell – tawny November. Under the trees, husks and hard fruits are furling and rotting. He waits. The pressure and temperature of the house changes, scents enter, great free gusts of coppice and bonfire and heath, and beyond, the city's miasma. It doesn't take long. Her head and shoulders come through the doorway. She pauses, one front paw lifted and pointing, her jaws parted, the folded tongue lifting up. He stares straight ahead. He tells himself it is not a choice. He does not want her to leave and yet he can no longer stand the lunacy, the impasse, his daily torment. Sophia has gone, he tells himself.

She bolts, a long streak of russet down the lawn, between the plum trees, and up over the fence, the white tip flashing like an afterthought.

He feels nothing. Not relief. Not sorrow. That night he leaves the back door standing open, love's caveat. In the morning there are slugs and silvery trails on the kitchen floor, sodden leaves blown in, and the bin has been knocked over. The following night he shuts the door, though does not lock it. His dreams are anguished, involving machinery and dogs, his own brutality, and blood.

*

Winter. A little snow, which gives England an older, calmer appearance. She has not come back. He worries about the cold, what might become of her, out there. There are distant nocturnal screams, like a woman being forced – are they hers? He checks the garden for signs, prints in the crisp skin of ice, her waste. The line he tells is one of simple separation. The neighbours do not ask further questions. A letter arrives from her place of work accepting termination of employment. All the while the enormity of what has happened haunts him. The knowledge might send him insane, he thinks. One day he will take off his clothes and lie in the street and beat his head with his fists and laugh as if choking. He will admit to killing her, beg for jail, though her body will never be found.

He returns to work. He is polite and, to new workers in the office, sullen-seeming. Those who know him, those who met his wife, understand some vital spark has been extinguished. He cannot quite reclaim himself. He feels victimhood strongly. Something has been taken from him. Taken, and in the absurdest possible way. He pities himself, abhors his passivity – could he not have done more? After a while it dawns on him that she doesn't want to come back, that perhaps she did not want what she had. An act of will. Her clothes hang in the wardrobe, until, one morning – the mornings are always easier and more decisive – he gathers them up, folds them carefully and places them in bags. He goes through the contents of her purse. They offer nothing enlightening, not even her lipstick, a red hue women can rarely wear, or the small purple ball, too gnomic to interpret. But these intimate items he cannot throw away. He places them in a bottom drawer.

Enough, he thinks.

He tries to forget. He tries to masturbate. He thinks of others, of partial, depersonalized images, obscenities; he concentrates, but release will not come. Instead, he weeps.

A week later, close to Christmas, he begins to walk on the heath again. That moulted protean place, which he has for months avoided. He walks at first light, when the paths are deserted, and the low red sun glimmers between bare twigs. He is not looking. He is not looking and yet he feels keenly aware of this old, colloquial tract of land, with its debris of nature, hemmed in by roads and houses, lathed away by bulldozers. It is fecund. It is rife with a minority of life-forms. Black birds in the stark arboretum, larval-looking and half-staged in the uppermost branches. The dead grass rustling. A flash of wing or leg. Sometimes he sits for a while, his collar turned up, his gloveless hands on the fallen trunk, whose sap is hard and radiant. His breath clouds the air. He is here, now. He would give himself, except there is no contract being offered.

He might find comfort in the sinew of winter, when nothing exists but that which is already exposed, and so he does, slowly, and as the earth tilts back towards the sun, his mind begins to ease a little. To be comfortable inside one's sadness is not valueless. This too will pass. All things tend towards transience, mutability. It is in such mindful moments, when everything is both held and released, that revelation comes.

So she appears on the path in front of him, in the budding early spring. He has been staring down at his feet as they progress, at the shivering stems and petals. All around him, the spermy smell of blossom. Yes, the world is saying, I begin. He looks up. The vixen is on a grass mound, twenty feet ahead. She is like a comet in the surroundings, her tail, her flame. She has her head lowered, as if in humility, as if in apology for her splendour, the black backs of her ears visible. Oh, her golden greening eyes. Her certainty of colour.

How easily she can fell him; and he will always fall.

She faces him. He waits to hear his name, just his name, that he could be made un-mad by it. She steps into the low scrub of the forest floor, takes a few high and tidy steps, and he thinks at first the wilderness has finally untamed her, she is afraid, about to run. But she turns, and pauses. Another step. A backward glance.

What, then, is she piloting? Is he to follow?

The old, leftover stretch of heath, preserved by a tenuous council ruling, by councillors who dine in expensive restaurants with developers, has a crock of boulders and hardwoods at its centre. Moss. Thrift. Columbine. Tides of lesser vasculars. She picks her way in, a route invisible to his eye, but precisely marked, it seems. Rock to stump, she crosses and criss-crosses. She knows he is following; his footfalls are mortifying, though he tries to tread respectfully through this palace of delicate filaments. He keeps his distance. He must convey at all costs that he has no intention to touch her, take her, or otherwise destroy the accord. The roots of old trees rear out of the ground, pulling strings of soil up with them. These are earnest natives; they have survived blight and lightning and urban expansion. They bear the weight of mythical, hollow thrones. Lungs of fungi hang from their branches.

Beneath one trunk there is an opening, a gash between stones and earth. Her den. She makes a circuit of the nearby copse, then sits beside the entrance, laying her flaring tail alongside her. Her belly is pinkish and swollen. She is thinner than he remembered, her legs long and narrow-footed, like a deer's. She cocks her head, as if giving him licence to speak. But no, he must not think this way. Nothing of the past is left, except the shadow on his mind. From her slender jaw she produces a low sound, like a chirp, a strangled bark. She repeats it. He does not know what it means. In their house she was never vocal, except with displeasure. Then, from the dark gape, a sorrel cub emerges, its paws tentative on the den-run, its eyes opaque, bluish, until only recently blind, a charcoal vulpine face. Another follows, nudging the first. And another. There are four. They stumble towards their mother. They fit to her abdomen, scrambling for position, stepping on and over each other. As she feeds them her eyes blink closed, sensually, then she stares at him.

Privy to this, no man could be ready. Not at home, skulling the delivery within the bloody sheets, nor in the theatre gown, standing behind a screen as the surgeon extracts the child. The lovely sting in him! They are, they must be, his. He crouches slowly. She is thirled to the task, but not impatient. Before they are done she nudges the cubs away. They nose against each other. They rock, vulnerably, on their paws, licking the beads of milk from each other. A great inspirational feeling lets loose in him. He has sweeping masculine thoughts. He understands his duty. He swears silent oaths to himself and to her: that he will guard this secret protectorate. That he will forgo all else. He will, if it comes to it, lie down in front of any digger before it levels this shrine.

The cubs remain above ground a moment longer. They play in silence, programmed to safe mutism, while she watches. They have her full attention. Their coats are dirty, sandy camouflage, but nothing will be left to chance. She curtails their crèche. One by one, she lifts them by their scruffs towards the hole, sends them back inside, and then, without hesitating, disappears after.

As he leaves he memorizes the way. The den is not as far from the path as he thought, dogs off their leads will detect their secretions, but it is secluded, lost behind a sward of bracken. She knows. His head is full of gold as he walks home. He allows himself the temporary glow of pride, and then relinquishes it. He has no role, except as guest. The truth is their survival is beyond his control.

He does not return every day, but once a week makes an early foray into the woods. He approaches respectfully, remains at a distance; a watcher, estranged. He never catches them out but must wait for an appearance. They materialize from the ground, from the undergrowth, an oak stump. If they know him they show no indication. Past a look or two – their eyes eerie and hazelish – they pay him no heed. Their mother has sanctioned his presence, that is all. The exclusion is gently painful, but it is enough to see them, to watch them grow.

And how rapidly they grow. The dark of their faces shrinks to two smuts either side of their noses. The orange fur begins to smoulder. Their ears become disproportionate. They are quick, ridiculously clumsy, unable to control their energy. He laughs, for the first time in months. Then their play turns savage, tumbling and biting. They learn to focus, peering at small moving quarry; they stalk, chew beetles, snap at airborne insects, while their mother lies in the grass, exhausted by them. She brings fresh carcasses, which they tug at, shaking their heads, twisting off strips of carrion. And still she feeds them her milk, though they are two thirds her size and he can see the discomfort of her being emptied, of manufacturing and lending nutrients. Sometimes she looks at him, as if waiting for his decision.

He is a man with two lives. He works, he holds conversations with office staff, shops at the supermarket. He turns down dates, but seems contented, and his colleagues wonder if he has, without declaration, moved on. Esmé is re-employed, though she is sad Sophia Garnett has left her husband and suspects injustice against her to be the cause – whatever that may be. But she finds no trace of any other woman in the house, no lace underwear, no lost earring or hairs gathered in the sink. The thoughts of murder pass.

He watches men lifting their children out of car seats and up from toppled bicycles. He watches them push swings. If anyone were to ask, he would say, I am not without happiness. He walks the heath. He monitors the landscape. He worries about the cubs, the multitude of dangers, even as they grow larger and stronger, and he can see all that they will be. They ambush their mother, who at times seems sallow, having sacrificed her quota of prey, having no mate to help her. They show interest in the rubbish of the woods, bringing back wrappers and foil, even the arm of a plastic doll. There will be dispersal, he knows, but not yet. For now, they are hers, and perhaps his, though peripherally.

One day an idea strikes him. He goes to the den site. They are not there, but he doesn't linger. He takes from his pocket the little purple ball Sophia used to keep in her purse. He places it by the entrance. The next time he comes it has vanished. He looks around until he finds it, lying under a thornbush nearby. He picks it up. There are teethmarks in the surface, scratches, signs of play.

What will become of them he does not know. The woods are temporary and the city is rapacious. He has given up looking for meaning. Why, is a useless question, an unknowable object. Who, will never be known. But to suspend thought is impossible. The mind is made perfectly of possibilities. One day, Sophia might walk through the garden, naked, her hair long and tangled, her body gloried by use. She will open the back door, which is never locked, and enter the kitchen and sit at the table. I dreamt of the forest again, she will say.

It is a forgivable romance, high conceit – he knows. At night he lies in bed, not at its centre, but closer to the midway point. He thinks of Sophia, the woman he loved. He no more expects her to return than he conceived of her departure. But he imagines her stepping across the room, bare, and damp from the shower. And then he thinks of the fox, in her blaze, in her magnificence. It is she who quarters his mind, she whose absence strikes fear into his heart. Her loss would be unendurable. To watch her run into the edgelands, breasting the ferns and scorching the fields, to see her disappear into the void – no – how could life mean anything without his unbelonging wife?

Case Study 2:
· Recognition of the Self ·

Referral and initial presentation

Christopher Surname Unknown
Born 22.02.2004

When Christopher arrived for his first assessment there were elements of 'wildness' to him – long unstyled hair, signs of tooth decay, brown patches on his skin from ringworm. Nor did he behave like a normal eight-year-old boy. He oscillated between stony emotional blankness and moments of high energy, when he prowled around the room, picking up objects and examining them with almost forensic scrutiny – he seemed especially drawn to the collection of ammonites and geological specimens I kept on the shelf. He had no concept of basic social restrictions and rules – for example he found the shoes he was wearing uncomfortable so he took them off and began to chew at one of his heels. When he spoke he used a fascinating and unorthodox mode of verbal communication, lacking the first person singular. 'We want to go back to Lea' was one of the first things he told me. Christopher was referred for treatment after hospitalization due to extreme weight loss. He was at that stage living in temporary foster care after removal from his home – a mountain commune called Brant Lea, near K-town, which is an isolated fellside settlement in Northern England.

Background

Christopher had been discovered wandering the upland moors by a hiker, disoriented and suffering from mild hypothermia, and was admitted to the paediatric ward of the local hospital. He was 18 kg (80 per cent of his expected body weight) and alarmingly cachexic – staff described him as 'looking like a child from a concentration camp'. He also had lice and fungal nail infections. There were no dental or immunization records. He displayed a highly restrictive eating pattern and when questioned he described his diet as consisting of produce grown or gathered by the commune – legumes, lettuce, wild snails, rabbit, and crayfish. The site was eleven miles from K-town, an old, part-ruined farm property on common land that the group had squatted in and taken over. Christopher had spent all his life to date there. After a programme of in-patient weight restoration (sedation and nasogastric tube were unnecessary) Christopher began to eat moderate portions of food. He was discharged and placed in foster care, while Social Services assessed the case. After four weeks his foster carer took him to see the family physician, concerned about repeated weight loss. She suspected that Christopher had been using food avoidance tricks, like hiding bits of meat in his clothing and under his bed. There were also boundary issues – he kept walking in on her while she was in the bathroom, even after instructions not to, and he did not respect her personal property.

Assessment

At the intake session Christopher did not mind being weighed but had trouble engaging with the assessment process for any length of time and found it difficult to answer questions about himself. The first thing he voluntarily said was, 'We want to see the snail farm.' He did not refer to his mother as 'mum' but would respond to her given name of Amber. While able to recognize meaningful and familiar individuals, Christopher had an incoherent and fragmented sense of self; he could not distinguish his identity from that of others, particularly those in the commune. There was some growth retardation and his reading skills were well below average. However, he showed no signs of possessing a distorted body image or suicidal tendencies.

On the Eating Attitudes Index he obtained low scores on the perfectionism and maturity fear subscales. He did, however, hold a set of strong beliefs about controlling his food intake, his role in the community, and the importance of pleasing the 'Firsts' (original commune founders). When I asked if not eating very much would please them, he replied, 'When we fast we have spinny dreams. Pascal and Jan say our dreams make us special. They see between us.' (Pascal was one of the Firsts and seems to have had a pseudo-shamanic role and influence over the group.) 'Isn't it the job of adults to make sure children get enough food to grow up strong?' I asked. Christopher seemed confused, as if the notion of hierarchy and responsibility had not occurred to him. 'We always eat the snails,' he said. He then, quite animatedly, described a system he had created for detoxifying snails – three days in a box sprinkled with oatmeal, followed by starvation for two days. 'We punch holes in the lid,' Christopher told me, 'or they die. If they still have dirt inside they give our tummies an ache and we throw up.' 'How many snails do you usually eat?' I asked. 'Two,' he replied. 'Two a day? Can't you have more? I bet there are lots of snails around?' Christopher shook his head and became agitated. 'We mustn't, we mustn't, we give two to us all,' he repeated. When he had calmed down again we discussed what was an appropriate amount of food for each meal. I showed him the food pyramid chart, which he took some interest in. He then became restive, got up from the chair and took from the shelf one of the South Dakota hoploscaphites that I'd unearthed during my last Rock Soc trip to America. He did not seem to understand that the object belonged to me or that his request to take it might be inappropriate. I was keen to develop the therapeutic alliance, and I said it would be fine to *borrow* the fossil if he promised to return it at the next session (I was rather nervous about the arrangement). Christopher agreed, but it was clear he did not really understand the notion of ownership.

History of presenting problem and family history

In the next session, the hoploscaphite was returned. Christopher asked me what the rock was surrounding it. 'Pierre Shale,' I replied. 'Is it rocky where you lived on the mountain?' Christopher thought for a moment. 'Limestone, granite, no sandstone.' I was impressed by his knowledge of the area around K-town, which I am also familiar with. He then said, 'Hamish knows about bad soil.' 'Who is Hamish?' I asked. 'Hamish does sex with us.' The use of the plural pronoun on this occasion was particularly disconcerting but by then I was more used to Christopher's enmeshment terminology. 'Who do you mean by us?' I asked. Christopher simply nodded. 'We don't like him better than Sam and Pascal though,' he said.

After the weigh-in, I asked Christopher to draw pictures of the people at the commune and name them. I asked again about Hamish's sexual relationship and he pointed to Amber. He was able to separate out the identities of fellow communers when encouraged to do so, but his immediate response was invariably to assume a position of naïve unification with other individuals, hence 'we had sex', 'our tummies ache'.

It is important to relate the environment in which Christopher was raised, and the chaos of his upbringing. Records and interviews revealed that there were about nine or ten people at the commune, who had been living for over a decade in prefabricated barns and yurt-like tents, with no electricity, except that intermittently provided by a diesel generator. The primary members – Firsts – were as follows: Christopher's mother Amber, Amber's brother Noel and her former boyfriend Sam, and Pascal (for visual reference see genogram, figure 1.1). Christopher had an older sister, Liana (age approx. fifteen), who left the commune a year before Christopher's hospitalization and removal into care. I shall return to this point as it is of significance. There were no formal structures demarcating filial or platonic roles, Christopher was regarded as a 'community child': he was not obliged to

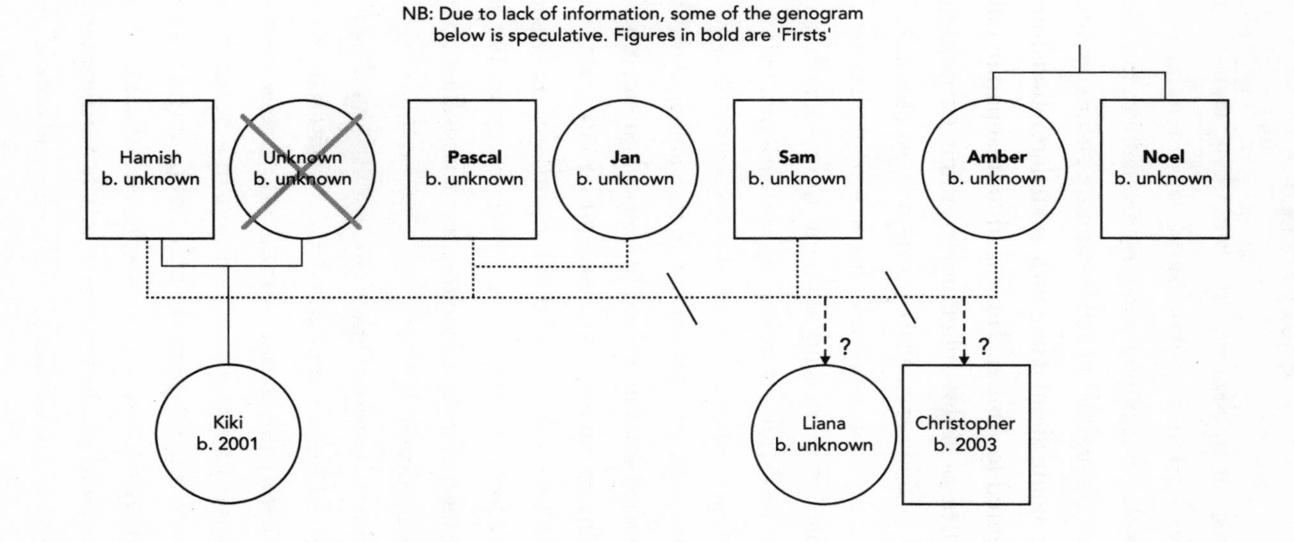

Figure 1.1 Genogram of Commune

sleep or eat in Sam and Amber's yurt, and his basic functions were not monitored with regularity. His home schooling appears to have been sporadic, though some of his practical skills were astonishing, for example he could tie fishing flies and knew how to work the generator, probably learned from watching those around him. Much of his time was spent autonomously, rather than with Amber, who was an unreliable figure and reacted to Christopher's needs erratically. For example, he related an incident where he fell through a barn roof and seriously injured his arm. When he approached Amber crying she continued singing the song she was playing on the guitar and ignored him. There were often extended periods when she was away from the commune with her brother Noel, trading at fairs. When I asked Christopher who he usually sought comfort from or help with a problem he said, 'We go to sleep and just wake up better. Sometimes Pascal sends a stroking dream.'

The community's ethos seems to have been one of brutal honesty and freedom. Meetings were held where everyone spoke, airing grievances, and disclosing feelings – both good and ill – towards other members. Secrets were regarded as damaging, as were positions of status and labels, though the Firsts seem to have held a certain prestige. Christopher told me that Pascal had originally seen the site in a 'flying dream' (perhaps under the influence of narcotics?) and the others had trusted him to find it. Christopher was excited by one genesis story in particular. Two of the commune's barns had been built by the Firsts. Complaints were made (one suspects architectural innovation was an excuse for people to complain about the group of settlers) and planning officers investigated. Since, one assumes, no permission had been granted, orders were given for the structures to be dismantled. The Firsts chained themselves to the doorframes. 'We stopped the diggers bashing our barns down,' Christopher told me proudly. 'But this all happened before you were born?' I suggested. 'Maybe Liana remembered it happening and told you about it?' But Christopher proved unresponsive to this character differentiation. He would often end the sessions prematurely, dead-eyed and without much emotion. On this occasion though he went to the shelf of fossils and lifted up a piece of fulgurite. After a few moments he said, 'It's too light.' I explained that fulgurite is created by lightning hitting sand, turning the sand into another substance. I asked him if he would like to take it home with him and bring it back again at the next session and he seemed pleased.

In the following assessment sessions the complicated and unboundaried nature of relations at the commune became more clear, as did the lack of stable and predictable parental care. Prior to Christopher's hospitalization there had been a period of intense disruption. First his sister chose to leave (he had no contact with her after her departure). Then Hamish (a recent widower) and his daughter Kiki (aged ten) joined the group. The loss of his sister, and the new arrivals, caused Christopher to feel agitated and confused. Soon after his arrival, Hamish formed a sexual relationship with Amber, which Christopher witnessed first-hand on several occasions: 'We didn't have to go outside if we didn't want to while there were the noises.' When I asked Christopher if Kiki liked living on the commune and was his friend, he said, 'No.' 'Why not?' 'Kiki doesn't share books and clothes. She doesn't come in the bath.' Christopher then described a large communal clay bath, which several members of the group used at the same time. The structure appeared to be primitive and was heated underneath by a wood fire. It seems Kiki also felt uncomfortable with the levels of nudity on the site and would remain clothed in Christopher's presence. On one occasion she had thrown sawdust in his eyes when he'd walked in on her using the toilet (there were no proper doors on the latrines). 'Our face stung,' he told me. The unstructured environment was rendered increasingly confusing by the arrival of father and daughter, whose general habits were not in keeping with anything he recognized as 'normal'. It was during this period that Christopher began controlling his food intake. He described eating a precise number of wild snails per day and avoiding meal times by hiding on the moors or pretending one of the other commune members had given him food. That Christopher was left to his own devices much of the time meant his condition either went unnoticed or was ignored. The Child Protection Enquiry report shows his mother's response to his hospitalization as follows: 'He's just a bony kid. He runs around so much. And he knows where the eggs are kept if he's hungry.'

Due to the complexity of the case, I felt it would be helpful to speak to Christopher's mother myself in order to assess his perception of life at the commune against hers, and to discuss the possibility of her attending treatment sessions. There is a contact mobile number but the first few times I rang no one answered. (There is a poor signal in the mountains around K-town.) Finally, I was able to reach Pascal. I introduced myself and asked to speak with Amber. Pascal was initially hostile and uncooperative, saying, rather defensively, 'What right have you got to interfere? You want to criticize our lifestyle, but what's your own life like? You can't see into him like we can. What do you know about children?' When I assured Pascal that talking to Amber would be of benefit to Christopher, and that Christopher's condition might permanently damage his health, he relented. It took a few minutes for Amber to be found and then she came on the line. 'I don't want to talk about Christopher,' she said. 'He made his choice and I respect that. But he's away from us now.' I tried to point out that her son was, at the time of leaving the commune, terribly underweight, sick, and disoriented, and his condition and age meant that he was far from being able to make rational decisions. I told her Social Care had intervened as a matter of routine. 'Intelligence isn't about age, those are just society's concepts,' she said. 'Christopher knows all about the environment and love. You want him to be selfish and a machine that only thinks about itself. You want him to be like you, but he won't ever be like you.' The conversation was deeply frustrating. Amber would not answer questions directly and obfuscated her points, either deliberately or because her thought process was disordered. When I asked, 'Aren't you interested in helping your child?' she replied, 'But he's not mine, he's ours.' When I asked if Christopher's father might care to attend the sessions, she hung up.

At this stage I found the case particularly difficult and stressful and asked my supervisor to review. I should note that I had recently separated from my partner over issues relating to starting a family – we were unable – and I felt that some of what was being discussed in the sessions was too close to the bone.

Christopher was painfully thin. He had no physical inhibition and he would often sit on the floor against my legs or touch my arms or my hair. It was distressing to think of his own mother being wilfully neglectful, and I found Amber's arrogance maddening. I was granted two weeks' leave, after which I resumed my work with Christopher.

Initial formulation

My impression of the commune was poor from the beginning and much of what was disclosed by Christopher and the conversation with Amber verified my suspicions. There was little privacy or coherence, and the culture, 'all of one mind and all free', which abdicated responsibility and parental leadership, and prized sexual openness and unboundaried sharing, provided an unstructured upbringing for Christopher. The inconsistent behaviour of his mother (and in fact all 'caregivers' he was exposed to) and her low levels of expressed emotion resulted in a highly ambivalent attachment style which was reflected in his ways of relating to both his foster carer and myself within our sessions. Never knowing what to expect from Amber and with a complete failure of consistent emotional recognition and mirroring, he was not able to know his own emotional state, wants and needs, or have them validated. I suspect that Christopher's perception was that, because those around him reacted purely in the moment to their own individual wants and needs, he had very little control over the external world. Such an inconsistent and confusing environment is likely to have had a highly detrimental effect on Christopher and at a young age he had no choice but to collude in the maladaptive schemas of the commune. His sense of self in large part failed to develop and my hypothesis was that he used methods of food control in an attempt to create order due to a chaotic internal state.

The aim of our sessions was therefore primarily to separate the individual self from the collective, to recognize personal and societal boundaries and to break the restrictive eating patterns. In essence, Christopher needed re-parenting in order to learn to recognize and understand his own internal state and develop a more functional attachment style now that he was to be integrated into mainstream society.

Initial treatment sessions

In the early sessions Christopher was often emotionally void, ignoring me or dismissing the conversation if he did not want to participate. He also spontaneously attempted to take his clothing off several times, kept opening and closing the window and disrupting the proceedings in other ways, and repeatedly expressed a desire to be sent back to the commune. He often wanted to curtail the early sessions, but as he became more engaged he began to throw tantrums. As I was drawing later sessions to a close, he occasionally needed to be forcibly removed by his foster carer.

Over the weeks of treatment he began to respond well to the environment of the foster home, with its predictability and boundaries, and over a five-month period his weight stabilized. He was able to follow simple house rules like knocking on a door before entering, and not attempting to get into the bathtub with other house members. The exercise of lending my fossils, though rather unorthodox, worked well as it encouraged a relationship of trust between us, while also illustrating the nature of ownership and personal possessions. I told Christopher where each fossil had been found – Syria, Argentina, North Wales – and why each was meaningful to me. Towards the end of treatment his carer indicated that Christopher had himself started to remember to return the items without her prompting. During my two-week leave I had travelled to Morocco, and on one paleo-mineral tour I found a beautifully preserved mid-Ordovician trilobite, which I decided to give to Christopher. The following session he brought it back. This time I had to explain that it was a gift, and now belonged to him.

More difficult was encouraging Christopher to use the first person singular, to begin to ask, 'Who am I?' and understand, 'I am me.' Progress in this area was painfully slow. Christopher believed himself to be somehow joined with the commune, and could not identify the single entity of himself, at least not consciously. Encouraging him to say 'I' instead of 'we' created high levels of anxiety – he often shouted, 'But we aren't alone,' and would scratch at his arms or hit his head. His fear of individuation was profound and induced panic and upset. It was as if he felt I was trying to convince him that he was becoming a new person, unknown, a stranger to himself, rather than acknowledging his existing state. I would often find myself embracing him in order to calm him down. As an intermediate stage, I began to get him to use his name to describe himself, thereby gradually demarcating his identity. 'How's Christopher today?' I would ask. 'Christopher watched *Batman* last night,' he would reply.

A breakthrough came during a project to replicate the snail farm. I was keen to have Christopher teach me how the process of detoxifying worked and thereby demonstrate his unusual skills. As Christopher was punching holes in the lid of the margarine box, I asked, 'Where will we get the snails from?' 'I can always find them hiding under leaves,' he told me. The moment passed without his noticing the self-referencing language, but it had a remarkable effect. In the following session his mood levelled, he became emotionally consistent and he was able to use the personal pronoun with greater ease. My own reaction to this breakthrough was to feel immense satisfaction, and I struggled to maintain my composure.

Outcome and updated formulation

Though seemingly physically healthy and responding well to psychological treatment, Christopher was found unconscious in his room in the foster carer's home on 25.01.2013. There was no sign of violence or sickness. He was pronounced dead after two hours of attempted resuscitation. Post mortem results were inconclusive, showing no sign of illness, trauma, or suicide. While the initial formulation was not incorrect, it is possible there was an underestimation of the strength of Christopher's attachment to the collective – one must leave room for the inexplicable. Due to the rare nature of the presenting case it was always my intention to publish it as a paper in the *Journal of Contemporary Child Psychotherapy* and I felt that the tragic outcome should not deflect me from this intention. On reflection, perhaps treatment proceeded too rapidly and a full range of risk-influencing factors were not identified and taken into account. The case is currently being reviewed as part of an ongoing Severe Untoward Incident investigation.

On a personal note, working with Christopher, though fascinating, was also extremely challenging and disturbing. At times I felt particularly angry towards his mother, my supervisor, and even my own limitations in helping him. I began to question my own boundaries. I wondered whether this was ultimately influenced by my childlessness, a state that I had until then believed myself to be reconciled with, and feelings of attachment to Christopher. I found his sudden death extremely confusing and could not come to terms with it. I spent weeks researching medical journals, looking for reasons he might have passed away, and I also made several visits to the K-town commune, but was never allowed inside, and on the last visit there was an altercation. I have since restarted my own personal therapy. Christopher's was my final case. I was granted six months' leave of absence from work, and following this I made the decision to retire permanently from practice.

· Theatre 6 ·

You are dreaming of geese, of all things. Geese in a field by a river. Grey geese, like the ones you pass on the cycle ride to and from the hospital. There are thousands, covering the grass. The geese have their heads raised, but their wings are splayed and crooked on the ground, as if broken. In the dream, you cycle very carefully through them, only just missing the tips of their feathers, the bicycle wobbling and tilting. The sound they make as you ride past is unholy, a sawing cry.

When your bleep goes it is ear-splittingly loud, thanks to its new battery. Geese, you think, as you come round. You reach over, fumble and drop the device, sit up and retrieve it from the floor. The on-call room is never dark enough, even with your eye-mask. White standby light from the computer flares slowly. The clock numerals on the wall opposite are faintly luminous.

Four a.m. You recognize the number on the bleep display. A & E. This is how it usually begins. You go to the phone on the wall, call the number. It takes a while for anyone to answer. The gynae registrar picks up. You recognize her voice, but can't for a moment think of her name.

Hi, I'm booking someone on the theatre list, she says. We need to get her up there now.

Yes, OK, you say.

Pregnant female, twenty-nine, foetal distress. Approximately twenty weeks. The mother is very unwell, probably started miscarrying a week ago. She was told by her GP to wait it out, you know.

Her voice is quiet, the tone uncomfortable, or annoyed, you can't tell which. Annoyed, you decide. There's a pause – and you can hear noises in the background, the flurry of activity in the emergency department, alarms, bustle, raised voices. Then the registrar says:

Blood pressure is a hundred over sixty, heart rate one thirty, temperature thirty-nine, maintaining sats. We're resuscitating. I've given her two litres of Hartmann's, and Tazocin. She's septic.

The last filaments of sleep disperse, and now you are alert.

She'll need more, you say. What IV access have you got?

I've got one eighteen-gauge in the antecubital fossa. She's quite difficult.

I'll come down, you say.

Yep.

The line goes dead.

You bleep the Operating Department Practitioner, Karen, who rings back immediately. You tell her to get everything together – someone's coming up.

What have we got, she asks.

Distressed pregnancy. Twenty weeks.

Right-o. Want me to notify the night officer or ask for a recorder?

You think for a moment. You have not yet seen the patient and the gynae registrar did not mention anything untoward. Karen is good, thorough, discreet. You've worked well together in the past.

No, you say. Leave it. Who's around up there?

Robin. And Jim.

Can you send Jim on a break?

I'll try.

The walk to A & E takes five minutes. The corridors glimmer dully underfoot and are empty mostly; you pass a porter and a woman sweeping the floors, Cley and Winterton wards. You pass the chapel. The lights are low; the small electric candles and crucifix on the altar are always lit. Above the doorway a sign reads *Life Is Sacred.* Sometimes you go into the chapel to sit, but not tonight. You focus on the forthcoming procedure. It will not be your decision, of course, the surgeon will prioritize, but you will be complicit – the entire team will be. Since the new legislation came in two years ago, the hospital has been fined several times, and a review is underway. You've already filled out several reports this year, and you've received a disciplinary letter, which, you are assured by several of your consultants, is simply a formality and can be disregarded. Among some, such a letter is a badge of honour. You are uncomfortably aware, though, that in other hospitals medics have been charged and struck off; their names listed on the back pages of the journals. One or two have even been attacked in the street.

You key in the code, push open the door of A & E and walk through the bays. There's the usual racket and pace, machines beeping, staff in motion – managed disorder. A bloody-faced drunk lolls on the edge of a gurney shouting obscenities. You wash your hands, ask a nurse where the theatre patient is. He gestures to a bed. The curtains are partially open but the woman is alone. Most of the staff seem to be attending a car crash victim at the far end of the room, where there is debris strewn on the floor, the residue of a shirt, a pair of cut-open jeans. The gynae reg has disappeared.

The pregnant woman is lying on her side, eyes closed, deathly pale and sweating profusely; the mound under the gown is wet. She has a hand tucked across her lower abdomen. There's a receptacle next to her on the bed into which she has vomited. You check the pressure bag is pushing fluids and read her chart notes. She opens her eyes, lifts her head, and looks up at you.

I'm Dr Rosinski, you say. I'm the anaesthetist registrar. I'm going to put another cannula in you, before we take you to theatre, is that OK?

With effort, the woman nods. Her head falls back on the pillow. You take gloves from a box on the wall, select a sixteen-gauge cannula. You tourniquet, tap and brush the forearm, find the cephalic vein and swab the skin with a steri-wipe.

Sharp scratch, you say.

The needle slides in. She doesn't flinch. She looks up at you. Her cheeks and chest are garishly flushed against the pallor.

I don't want – she whispers. Please, don't let me –

She is trembling and cannot say it. You can see fear in her eyes, under the disorientation of illness and shock, fear that used to be selfless, but is now for herself as well as for the baby. Such cases are common enough not to make the newspapers anymore.

I know, you say, gently. It'll be OK.

You can't really say more. What could you say? Our surgeons are excellent. Our maternal mortality rates are among the lowest in the country. *We don't all believe in the Hunter foetal care plan.* You finish cannulating. You take a blood culture and gas, complete the anaesthetic assessment, tape over her rings, then find a nurse and a porter to help wheel the bed. On the way to theatre the patient vomits again. The sheet underneath her is stained and her breathing has become more laboured.

Don't worry, the nurse says, daddy is on his way, I'm sure. And the baby will be just fine.

Inane, soothing and a lie. Or perhaps the nurse is simply playing her part; it is hard to know sometimes. You wonder – if everybody acts with duplicity, do they arrive at a kind of truth? But you say nothing, certainly not the obvious. That the patient is beyond such things now. That if the products of conception are not evacuated fast, the infection could become fatal. *Products of conception* is not a permitted term anymore. Nor *septic abortion*. There is a new language, which must be written, if not spoken. *Pre-birth crisis. Unsalvageable uterine life.* You've seen this level of disintervention before – the extraordinary bleeding and blossoming of bacteria, which amounts to neglect. God's Jurisdiction, is how the prime minister described it in his speech to parliament. He is a great orator, they say, the best for decades.

The woman is crying softly. You would like to give her something more, ketamine, temazepam, but the options have been limited. If on the drug chart it appears you are disregarding the baby's health, even at this stage, it will look bad. At the lifts you thank the nurse and say you and the porter can manage the rest of the way. The nurse smiles, reaches into her pocket and takes out a small silver disc, on which there is an embossed angel. You've seen these items on sale in the hospital gift shop – twenty pence each – they're found all over the wards and in the chapel's votive plates. The nurse presses the icon into the hand of the patient.

Thank you, you say. I'll have to take it off her before surgery, but I'll put it somewhere safe.

You press the button and the lift doors close.

In the Anaesthetics Room Karen has thoughtfully brought you a cup of tea. It's lukewarm. There's no time – you take two sips and bin it. You wash your hands. You and Karen transfer the patient to the table. You check the ID band again, position her head and neck so she is *taking the morning air.* You give her 100 per cent oxygen, push the milky hypnotic, and paralyse. After sixty seconds you remove the mask, Karen hands you the laryngoscope, you view the cords, and intubate. You scrub your arms, to the elbow. You place a central line as swiftly and smoothly as you ever have. Then you wheel her into Theatre 6 and attach her to the ventilator. They are all waiting, masked and gowned. The gynae reg has scrubbed in; she nods to you. Dr Malhotra – now you remember her name. She was there last year, during the Hannah Lehrer surgery, which is now the Hannah Lehrer case. You do not recognize the consultant. He introduces himself.

Hello. I'm Mr Desai.

You introduce yourself, Karen and the support worker do the same, the nurses. The WHO checklist is repeated. You adjust the table upwards, and the patient is positioned.

Are we without a night officer? the surgeon asks.

I believe so, you say.

You catch Karen's eye for the briefest moment before she looks away.

And are we recording?

No. Our tech is on a break.

OK then, let's get going, Mr Desai says; his tone light, almost sing-song.

He steps towards the table.

May I have your permission to disinfect? he asks, peering at you above his glasses and mask.

He is politer than most consultants, the politeness of absolute confidence, perhaps. Drapes are being placed around the patient.

Please go ahead, you say.

As the surgeon sterilizes, he glances at you again and says:

It's a nice bike.

Excuse me, you reply, thinking you've misheard.

Your Peloton. It's a nice bike. I used to have one. I saw you putting it into the rack yesterday evening.

Oh, right.

Cycle in every day?

Yes. Most days. I live in Chesterton.

Ah, good for you. I would, but I live too far out now. My wife likes to be in the countryside. Which way do you come in?

Along the river. Past the crem.

Ah, beautiful, he says. Of course, that's the best way to come. Reminders.

He then asks, as courteously, for permission to begin. There are no ciphers and codes by which to discuss politics or protocol, perhaps these things are discussed without you realizing it, perhaps you even discuss them without realizing it. You monitor the anaesthetic machine, push intravenous antibiotics. Four litres of fluid. You start colloids, administer little boluses of metaraminol. The surgeon evacuates quickly, pronounces its time of death and notes its sex, which is a legal requirement. The drapes are soaked, dark. The patient's legs are lowered. Her blood pressure drops to sixty over thirty and sticks there – you have a sweaty few minutes getting it back up. You give her more fluids, noradrenalin, and begin a blood transfusion.

She's not enjoying this at all, you say.

A laparotomy kit is brought forward. The initial cut is vast. The surgeon and registrar converse calmly as they operate. They attempt to save, and then remove the woman's uterus. Finally, Mr Desai steps back, and Dr Malhotra closes, as carefully as stitching the hem of a wedding gown. You and Karen wheel the patient into recovery. She is extremely pale, but alive. She is lucky, though under what order of providence you could not say.

The anaesthetist for the next shift arrives and begins the handover. You tell him about the night's procedure.

Christ. Glad I missed that hot potato, he says. Another letter, right?

You shrug. You pass on the theatre list for the day – a ureteric stent, a bowel obstruction, revision of breast augmentation, nothing complicated. You are supposed to complete the requisite paperwork immediately and file a report to the Department for the Protection of Unborn Children, but instead you change out of your scrubs, go to the bike racks and head home. You've done your duty, enough.

The morning is clear, a few high clouds banking on the horizon. Dawn has come and gone, but it still feels fresh and damp and clean. You cycle through the hospital grounds, past the crematorium and across a small park, then along the river. The field is empty. The grass glistens under the wheels of your bike. When you look up there is a long dark vee of birds in the sky, migrating south.

· Wilderness ·

They climbed up the beach and onto the old railway tracks that ran round the headland. The tracks were overgrown and rust-wrecked, though the Outeniqua Choo Tjoe had been defunct less than a decade. Loose stones had fallen from the cliffs, landing in the cooked bitumen between pilings, and sticking there as the tar congealed. The three of them walked in a row, stepping on the broken laths, a few paces apart – Zachary leading, Joe next, then Becca. Above them was a grey Southern Cape sky that looked, Becca thought, entirely exportable to England. Down below, a big, upset sea – Cape sea, with Antarctic muscle behind it. They walked with heads down, their anoraks crackling. After a while, conversation got up about fears and phobias. Heights. Needles. Being shot in the back of the head in the cinema. Clowns' mouths.

Clowns' mouths?

Joe snorted. He paused a moment on the track, so Becca had to stop too, then carried on.

Don't you mean just clowns, Zach? The whole clown entity is considered pretty sinister.

I do not, mate, Zachary said. I mean exactly their mouths. Their lipsticky mouths. Like giant red vaginas.

Joe snorted again, the snort of the incredulous. Becca said nothing. She had been saying nothing most of the morning. Zachary mustn't have seen many vaginas, she thought, though his wife was extremely beautiful, in a strange Martian way. Lizette was an ex-Boden model, who'd gone religious after pushing out two of Zach's kids. She had long black hair down to her backside, upholstered lips and hipbones that jutted out of her jeans like scaffolding. She'd made Becca feel inelegant and very uncomfortable when they'd met the day before, though there was also a weird mental crackle off her.

Zachary himself was tall and fat. The kind of solid torso fat a man prefers to call barrel – barrel-chested or barrel-bellied, conjuring images of leopard-clad circus strongmen or Saxons. How he'd gotten Lizette to say yes, Becca couldn't guess. Ace in bed, maybe. Or a good sense of humour, though so far Zachary's prevailing mood was melancholia bordering on despair. There seemed to be a perpetual argument going on between the couple – she nagging him to take off his raggedy woollen hat, which he never did, or fix his strained-against belt, or not slurp his beer; sarcasm circling around everything he said to her, mocking her accent or her lack of intellect. It was painful. Their house, where Becca and Joe were staying for a few days, was ramshackle for the poshed-up Garden Route. Zach and Lizette lived in the hills, which was half the price of living on the beach in Wilderness, apparently. She'd decorated the living room in vivid Mexican greens and attempted some Gauguinesque nudey murals on one wall. The women's breasts were asymmetrical, more like Picasso.

It's because they're around children. It's the paedo aspect, Joe was saying.

He'd stopped walking again suddenly and was gesticulating. Becca stopped too.

Subterfuge, he continued. They have big floppy feet and silly honk-honk noses, but what's behind the mask is a man who can't get proper work. So he has to resort to going to screaming kiddy parties twice a week. It's supposed to be a stopgap. But he never looks for another job. Bottom line is he enjoys frightening children.

No, no, no, said Zach. It isn't an abuse thing, Joseph. I didn't get fucking fiddled. You can knock that idea right out.

Zach kicked a loose stone on the tracks. It skittered ahead, curved left, and hopped over the cliff edge.

OK. Well it's Shakespearean then. Sadness and truth behind the comedy. Feste and Lear. Who is the fool? Psychology. Think about it, Zachary.

No, no, no, said Zach. It's their mouths, I'm telling you. It's the giant red lips.

Below, the ocean hoved in and exploded against the cliff base. Vapour drifted upwards smelling of rotten crustaceans and tonic water.

Maybe it's *It*, Becca said.

Zach leaned out, seaward, and looked around Joe.

What's that, hon?

It. The killer clown film. Sharp teeth. Jaundice. Stephen King. Maybe you're thinking of him?

He shrugged.

Haven't seen it. I don't like horror.

Zachary's a gargantuan poes, said Joe.

Oh, that's nice, boknaaier.

The boys – men as they were – had been bickering this way for two days. Becca didn't know any Afrikaans, because Joe didn't speak it usually. He and Zach had known each other since school in Pretoria. They were maybe even best friends. But the testiness between them sounded real, she thought, not fun banter, so something else was going on. She'd known Joe for six months and back in England he had seemed pretty relaxed. Here, home, he was different.

Up ahead a tunnel had been blasted through the cliff. There was a little white hole at the other end, maybe a few hundred metres away; it was hard to tell. Zachary stopped walking and took a joint out of his pocket. He tried to light it, but the wind was all-directional.

See, said Joe. Afraid of the dark. Big poes.

Bats, man, said Zach.

There are no bats in there.

Not the flying variety.

Zach crouched down behind a bush until the flame took and the spliff began to smoulder. He was growing the stuff in the garden and selling it to friends who took it back to Cape Town, mostly to the university. He and Lizette were saving to send the kids to private Catholic school, he'd said, to explain the bad little enterprise. But the stuff he was on with now, that he'd been on fairly persistently with since Joe and Becca had arrived, was pruned from a reef of plant growing wild on the mountain, a more potent species. They'd all had some the previous night after the kids had gone to bed. Lizette had smoked too, despite her religiosity, or maybe it was OK because it was God's own weed. Then she'd gotten weepy about her life and talked about how she was nothing now, and how Jesus was forgiving her for what she'd been before. The crimes were unspecified. Marrying Zachary, maybe, or getting banged by multiple Boden photographers at the age of sixteen.

The mountain bud had been damp and sticky, unlike anything Becca had tried before. It'd kept going out, but when lit it was head-slammingly strong. Fugueinducing. After a minute Becca felt like her eyes were melting. Time felt so slow she could write a song in her head between everyone's sentences, then it sped up and almost a year passed while she was trying to ask where the toilet was to be sick. A full-blown whitey; it was like being a teenager again.

She stepped towards the cliff wall and leant against the rock. Heights: that was her phobia. Some nights she dreamt of falling, falling and falling endlessly. The shooting in the head thing was Joe's; she didn't quite know what it meant about him. Some kind of trust issues? She didn't like standing still on the cliff – moving was much better than not moving, but the boys were now occupied with the smoke. Joe took the joint off Zach, pinched a cat's anus with his mouth and inhaled. He held it in, and exhaled theatrically.

Kif Dagga, Zachster.

Ja. Got to dry it out more, but the kids keep coming in the workshop and asking, what is that funny moss, Dah? Fucking Rufe is like Poirot.

You want some, Becs? Joe asked. Take the edge off the edge?

He laughed dumbly at his own joke. She shook her head. The walk was pretty scary. The ledge wasn't that narrow; whoever had laid the track had at least followed a sensible engineer's manual, but the drop was sharp enough to make her stomach pitch each time it became truly apparent. She didn't want to float off. She breathed in the marine air. The boys squabbled about clowns again for a minute until the argument became ridiculous and ended.

Come on, Becs, said Joe. Don't you want some for crossing Kaaimans?

She shook her head.

No.

It's pretty fucking high.

It's not that high, man, said Zach.

She'd been warned about the bridge when they were deciding which walk to do that morning. The Kaaimans river viaduct. It was famous. Zach had shown her a picture online – a big, leggy-looking structure with an old piston train crossing it, the passengers leaning out of the windows waving, billows of jolly steam above. Below the structure was a wide estuary. It didn't look that high, so she'd said she could manage it. Lizette hadn't wanted them to do the walk. She had a thing about the viaduct. The kids were forbidden to go anywhere near.

It's a devilish place, she'd said. You should walk on the beach.

Devilish? Don't be a crazy bitch, Zach had told her.

Moenie so met my praat voor Jesus en vreemde mense nie, she'd replied.

After that she'd refused to speak in English.

That's just fucking rude, ja, Zach had yelled. Becca's from London.

Yorkshire, Becca had said.

The kids, at separate ends of the house, had sensed domestic pressure mounting like barometers, and had started crying independently of each other. Zach had gone to the little girl's room, his wife had gone to lie down, and Rufus had stormed out into the garden with a toy and started pathologically bashing the windows with it. A long walk was essential.

Becca looked back along the coast towards Wilderness. The hills unwound, green and bluegreen. There were enormous rock buttresses, crescents of sand in the interstices. New houses were being built along the shorefront, huge modern boxes geometrizing upwards among the old gables. Driving past the beach on the way to the train tracks Zach had pointed out structures that were contravening planning laws, which he was officially protesting. His big arm hung outside the car window like a gangster's.

This one has paved over all the old milkwoods. Three-hundred-year-old milkwoods, and the guy tips a ton of concrete down like a total moron.

A few houses later:

This one has built a patio onto public beachfront. It's public beachfront. It belongs to the public. The guy is trying to get heavy with me. He's come up the mountain a few times in his larnie four-wheel-drive yuppie fucking aeroplane and parked in front of the house. Like that heavy shit's going to work, right. Banker. Thirty-seven and retired. Who retires at thirty-fucking-seven, hey? Who needs a three-storey house?

You always were a pedantic dick-swing, Zachary, Joe had said.

No, no, no. We might be a corrupt nation, Joseph, my friend, but someone has to point out the truth to these Towners. No one owns the sea. I'm challenging every single one of them, all the right channels, so they can't just pay someone off.

He was still pointing accusingly in the direction of the offending residence. Joe laughed.

Yeah. They have to go to court and then pay someone off.

Maybe, Zach said, bringing his arm back inside the car. We'll see.

They'd driven on. Then he'd braked hard, throwing them forward off their seats, and had reversed back fifty metres or so.

This one. This clever shit cut down the dune brush to get a better view. It's a protected species. Now his house is being eaten by sand, so he's building a fifteen-foot arsehole's Perspex wall – a Perspex wall!

And so on.

*

They passed the joint back and forth. Becca moved as close to the edge as was bearable and looked down at the water. Waves kept coming. Spume leapt up then dropped away in frothy white clods. The wind sailed around her legs. It was, as her granddad would have said, a narky bit of coast. She stepped back. How hard could it be to walk across a railway bridge, devilish or otherwise? She looked down the tracks. Ten years' disuse, but it seemed longer. Where they were standing the ties had been pried up and removed. There were small orange flowers embedded in the rock soil, flickering in the breeze.

Becs, said Joe. Look. You are really not going to like the crossing. After the tunnel we can go back. Zachster, we should go back after the tunnel, ja?

She'll be all right, man, said Zach. I take the kids over it all the time. Rufe walks it backwards like me.

Joe snorted again. The snorting was becoming a habit.

I know he does and I wish he wouldn't. It makes me incredibly nervous.

You just don't like Kaaimans yourself, Joseph. Confess.

Zach was smirking. Joe held up his hands. His two pinch fingers smoked.

That's because I'm not a death-wish psychopath,

like you. That thing's going to come down one day. Piece of creaking junk.

It's fine, Becca, said Zach. Don't worry, there's a handrail and everything.

Joe's snort was a kind of horrible, snorking, mucal sound. It was driving her mad.

Yeah, right. There's a handrail on a hovering platform separate from the actual fucking bridge – you have to squirrel along it like a yellow-foot!

Zach held up his hands too.

Hey, that is not cool, you're freaking your lady out. It's really safe, Becca. No one's fallen off, like, ever. Not even on purpose.

He put a hand on his woollen hat and rubbed it back and forth against his head, scratching the scalp underneath, then straightened it over his brow. Joe held out the joint.

You want some for the bridge, Becs? Go on.

She shook her head.

No.

He passed the joint to Zach. The coiled cardboard gerrick was damp and loose. Zach scrubbed it out on the wall, then flicked the stump off into the sea.

Oh, shit, he said, under his breath. It's a crackhead. Swerve.

Joe and Becca turned to look. A man was walking up the tracks behind them. He was tall and thin, the brilliant, salt-scoured thin of driftwood, nothing left on him but hard knots. He was wearing combat shorts and a navy waistcoat, old military boots strapped up his shins. He was swinging a see-through plastic carrier bag with something dark and smeary inside. They watched him approach and stepped aside to let him pass.

Howzit, Zach said.

Oh, fine, fine, the man replied. Beauty, yes, indeed. I've got mine here, thank you.

He shook the bag and the thing inside chunked about. His eyes were bright without any kind of reason, and slid off everything as soon as making contact. He was gurning a big smile, the teeth brown and gapped. As he passed by Becca got a big crackly feeling off him, a whiff of ancient sweat, and something foisty-smelling, like wet fur. For a moment he looked like he might stop and deal out some nonsense, but instead he shook the bag again, muttered something, and carried on up the tracks. The dark of the tunnel swallowed him. There was a pause, then Joe said:

Great. Is he going to knife us if we go in there?

Stop with your relentless anxiety, man, said Zach. You're killing my mellow.

Well, I'm giving that guy a wide berth.

Right, and I'm the poes?

They waited a little while and then went into the

tunnel. For a moment it was total pitch; Joe said a few echoey woahs. They walked slowly and the darkness softened until Becca could see the sloped walls of the tunnel, the glimmer of track and silver graphite particles. Their feet crunched on the clinkery floor. There was no sea sound. Now and then came a hollow fluting noise, like someone blowing across a bottle top. She could smell coaly deposits on the surfaces, cordite, paraffin, like fireworks in the park on bonfire night, or northern streets in December. Soot. Christmas.

She suddenly missed Whitby, with its tides of goths and lopsided abbey and sad little fishing fleet, though she'd been in London the last five years, struggling with the band. Nostalgia could come on her momentously, it had been coming on her a lot since she'd left with Joe, and it came on her now, made her want to turn and run. South Africa had been a mistake. Prospects here were no better, even though Joe had said they would be, that there'd be cool influences, and that it was cheaper to live. A musical odyssey, he'd said. The country was as tense as a nail, there were rules about race and language that she didn't understand, and Joe was either angry or stoned.

So far the road trip hadn't been fun. Shortage of funds meant they were mostly staying with friends of Joe's along the way: all of them were stressful to be around, except Kavi, a drummer from Durban whom Becca found very attractive, to the point of a near miss in his kitchen when Joe was passed out one night. There hadn't been much songwriting, like they'd planned. The sex was a bit dull, Joe kept trying not to use condoms, and he was a really bad driver. He'd driven them over an insane mountain pass in the Little Karoo. The road had been a joke, wall-less and untarred. Sheer canyons of red stone dropped thousands of metres and stacked red pinnacles rose, like something out of Middle Earth. After begging him to slow down she'd shut her eyes and resorted to singing her comfort song in her head, usually reserved for the dentist and flying.

The railway tunnel had a strange industrial eeriness, a primed feeling, like its memory of trains hadn't faded or it was convinced trains were still coming. The clinker ground underfoot like old bones. She looked back a few times towards the entrance and tried to judge their progress. Halfway. Two thirds. The central section was dark enough a man might be crouched in the shadows, or flush against the walls. Now she was getting paranoid. She reached out for Joe's arm but didn't make contact. Joe and Zach were squabbling about phobias again, their voices bouncing off the walls.

It's instinctive stinctive when you think think. Maybe we even evolved volved from being nocturnal urnal. Fear of the dark ark ark is because we've forgotten.

Evolution! Volution! Lution! The first person was black ack ack. What's that, that – camouflage arge?

The tunnel opening began to throw brightness inside and the wind blurred past Becca's face. Her eyes started to readjust. There were no figures lurking. They emerged into unglazed, grey daylight. Up ahead the tracks rounded the spur of the headland and disappeared. The boys were still at it.

It doesn't count if your eyes are shut and your brain is on standby. You can't be afraid if you aren't conscious.

Goat shit. You can be afraid in a nightmare.

That doesn't count. It can be broad daylight in the nightmare, man.

What?

Like you're dreaming of an animal chasing you, getting really close, big beak, hideous nails, like some kind of wyvern, but it's the middle of the afternoon . . .

What the fok is a wyvern?

Becca wanted to yell at them both to shut up. Just have a fight, or kiss, do something other than blether on. To the right was a large cave cut in the cliff, or maybe partly natural. Candles were placed at the entrance and puddled from use. Plastic furniture teetered on the uneven platform of rocks at the cave mouth, bistro-style, a broken table and chairs. The thin carrier-bag man was standing outside the entrance talking with another man, a horrendous man, even more gaunt, who looked like he'd been resuscitated from the cemetery. His face was almost skull, and there was a hanging garden of scrotum-like skin on the side of his neck. Some kind of tropical disease. A yellowed T-shirt hung from his collarbones.

Howzit, Zach said, and kept walking.

Joe and Becca followed and said nothing. The men stopped talking and stared at the passers-by, then at the table top, where a brown furry mass was lying in its own gross leakage. A matted tail dangled over the edge. After they'd passed by, the men began calling out.

Hello, bless you! Hello, bless you!

The calling went on a few seconds.

Bless you, hello, bless you!

Becca hurried after the boys.

What do they want?

Money, said Zach.

Was that a cat?

No doubt, hon.

Probably a dassie, Joe suggested.

It looked like a cat, she said. It had a tail.

Zach sniffed and nodded.

Ja. When those nutters are not cracking their tits off and remember they have stomachs they'll eat anything. I mean *anything*. Towners are always complaining about pets going missing. But since they let them run around and shit on the beach, what do they expect. They've got a petition to clear these guys out.

Do they live in that cave? Becca asked.

In winter.

Jesus, she said.

For a moment Zachary looked forlorn.

Welcome to Wilderness.

They got a nice view though, said Joe. Better than those rich bastards down there.

Becca sighed. Her boyfriend could be, no, he was, a total twat. She knew it. She looked back down the tracks but the cave-dwellers had moved inside and their dinner table was empty.

They rounded the headland and the wind whipped up. A wide yellow estuary gaped before them; rusty streaks of orange ran up along the sides of the river. Below, the water looked so shallow that the brains of fish would have to be flat. Light shone patchily on the surface, turning the water chemical green, bronze, aquamarine. And there was the viaduct – raised on stocky concrete legs, spanning the valley like a giant prehistoric centipede.

Kaaimans, said Zach, proudly, as if introducing an esteemed colleague.

Joe groaned.

Oh, man, I fucking forgot! Here we go again.

How many times have you crossed it? Becca asked.

He's done it twice, said Zach. And I assure you, it was an ordeal for me both times.

You all right, Becs? asked Joe. We can go back if you want.

She said nothing. It was too late, it was all much too late. They kept walking down the tracks towards it. Becca ran some quick panicky calculations. The viaduct didn't look that high. It didn't look that long. Less than five minutes to cross, perhaps. Lower than Blackpool Tower, and she'd seen kids in the Greek islands making bigger dives off the cliffs, maybe. She squinted and focused on the train tracks and tried not to think about what would shortly be either side and below – air, nothing, the drop. The trick was not to look down, obviously, and to take normal, confident steps, like walking on any normal confidence-inspiring surface. And not to stop. Stopping was like admitting something bad. She'd made that mistake before on mountain ridges, pausing at a teetery bit only to get vertigo and seize up – knees, knuckles, brain, all functions in lockdown. Joe didn't understand the feeling. It was a physical thing, like a migraine or stomach flu, hard to explain to anyone who hadn't had it.

They approached the beast. Lizette was right, something about the viaduct was disturbing, diabolical even. The iron girders were gory with rust; rust was bleeding profusely out of the bolted panels and leaking down the concrete legs into the river. It was divided into two sections, a wider bit where the train tracks ran over collapsing lattices of wood, and a slender flying walkway attached by cantilevers to the main platform, with, Zach hadn't lied, a handrail. The structure looked riven apart in the middle and waves could be seen rolling between. Zach stepped onto the walkway, easy-osy. Becca took a breath and followed. Commit, she thought, don't think about it, commit.

We really don't have to do it, Joe said. Becster?

She ignored him.

I don't want you to freak out.

She said she's fine, Zach said. He was ten feet out now and casually strolling along as if through a summer meadow.

Don't want an episode, like on the Swartberg pass, Joe called.

That was your bloody driving! Becca snapped.

Zach turned round and laughed.

Too fucking right, hon. He drives like bees are up his arse.

He took his hand off the rail and swarmed his arms about, making a buzzing noise. Becca kept her head in a neutral position, not up, not down, and tried to hold everything loosely in her peripheral vision – the grey sky, the rolling tide, the lurid streaky sandbars. Zach was holding his backside and prancing about. She wanted to shout at him to hold the handrail properly, stop fooling about. She didn't know how far behind Joe was – there was no possibility of her turning to see; forward gear was the only option.

Becs? Joe called.

She carried on walking, careful steps, balletic poise, denial of state. She was trying to remember the lyrics to 'Mr Sandman', but her mind was blank. All around was air, airiness. Beneath her feet the entire edifice of Kaaimans was corroding. There were ragged holes where rust had eaten through the metal, and some of the plates were missing – she had to keep stepping over gaps. The tide was playing visual tricks, rolling underneath, white-crested, fast, unmooring everything. The estuary was a series of chicaning rivulets. The wind got up a little, and she felt the giant structure vibrate and purr. Suddenly it made a hollow, horning sound, a kind of moan.

Jesus Christ!

She clutched the rail with both hands. Don't stop. She carried on, half twisted, letting go only when she had to, and quickly groping for purchase again. Where was her comfort song? Where was any song she knew? Her nose was running, she could feel a slick on her top lip – no chance of wiping it. There was space everywhere, vast and open. She kept going. She was breathing faster, shallower, but she was moving. They'd nearly reached the middle of the viaduct.

Becs, everything all right? How's it going?

Joe's voice sounded far away. Good. She wanted not to hear him. Not to know he was there. But now Zach was turning around again. He was turning around like he had acres of room under his feet and he was walking backwards – *backwards* – so he could see Becca and Joe's progress. Nausea rose in her – a sort of spastic fury. The idiocy! The carelessness! If she saw him fall, if he fell into the void, arms and legs flailing, tumbling and spinning, or if he fell still as a stone, dropping straight down, plummeting, then she would know exactly how it felt, she would feel the falling too. Kinaesthesia it was called – she'd had it before. A long time ago. When she'd seen someone go over the fence, on the grassy stretch near the abbey, on the crumbling cliffs . . . Or was it her, she was so small, she couldn't remember, just what they'd told her after. That someone had jumped off the Plain, a woman. And Becca had been found down on the beach too. Had she fallen? Or climbed down, to try to find whoever had gone over? Not a scratch on her. But the tide was coming in and the hem of her dress was wet. She'd dreamt of it so many times.

And soon she would be falling again, down, down, onto the hard, wet, thumping sand.

Waves sluiced through the concrete legs of the viaduct. Wind flushed in from the ocean. The metal structure keened its mournful note again. Zach was walking backwards, like he didn't care, like a man walking off the end of the world, ready to go. His face was peaceful, impervious.

Everything was loosening. Her grip. Her knees. The air. Even the viaduct was softening. The viaduct was floating free, and sailing on the wind. It was moving into the valley, into the river's mouth. It was going to hit the hillside, and heave and tip and buckle. The adrenalin was going in Becca's chest now, ping, ping, ping against her ribs . . . Her footsteps were getting clumsier; she couldn't control her muscles. Something inside her head tilted and spilled and that was that. She held the rail tight with both hands, and stopped.

No. I'm. Not.

All around and underneath the view rushed and wobbled. The atoms of things were going wrong. Her eyes were flooding.

Zach paused. He was twenty feet away, maybe; it was hard to tell. She blinked tears out. He waved. Was he waving?

Becca, he called.

She shook her head.

No.

Becca. Nearly there. Yeah?

She was barely breathing and then breathing hard. She was producing involuntary sounds as she breathed out. Mewls. Lows. Zach scratched his head with his hat. Or was he waving again?

Becca, he called. Nearly there. Are you coming on?

She blinked more tears. A gull flew by, very close, black feathers in the crook of its wings. It held still against the wind for a moment, cocking its head this way and that, while everything rushed. Its eye was yellow with a red ring. Disgusting. It looked at her, knew what she wasn't, then fell into a stoop towards the estuary. She shut her eyes, and felt the true, inglorious ride of the viaduct. It was gaining speed. Any moment now it would hit and tip and she would be falling, spinning away. She waited. She waited, for the slam, the blackness, nothingness, whatever dreadful thing was coming.

When she opened her eyes Zach was much closer – arm distance away. His hand was resting on the rail. His sleeve flapped in the breeze. He was talking softly, speaking Afrikaans, and then English. He didn't look like himself. He was saying something about Lizette and the cave-dwellers. Something about Bibles. The words flew past Becca and disappeared. Zach stepped forward without making a sound. He was very close now. Don't touch me, she thought, but he didn't touch her. He was still talking. She couldn't really hear, and she couldn't understand him. He was saying something about Lizette's dark habit, about getting down on her knees. He was saying things that didn't make sense.

Some days it would be better if we were all gone. Ja? As dit net wou end kry . . .

The words blew away. Zach's face blurred again. She blinked and it came into focus. Expressionless. He wasn't really Zachary. He was some kind of agent. He took a slow step back. Between them was the sea. Waves kept coming, white-tipped, the same, the same, the same, as if the water was an amnesiac. All seas were a single sea, they all joined. The sea had made her dress wet. It was all right to be sad when someone died, that's what her foster parents had told her, even someone you hadn't known. Like the young woman who'd left the baby on the cliffs, before she jumped.

Becca's hands ached from clenching the rail. They were grotesque and locked tight. With huge effort she straightened her fingers. Then she moved them a fraction along the rail. She pushed one foot forward and shuffled. Zach stepped away again as she moved. He was still talking, saying things she didn't understand. Forwards and backwards; they were crossing together. It took a long time. Forever, or just a few minutes, she couldn't tell.

The end of the viaduct was there, solid ground, a life – if she could get to it. She couldn't hear Joe. Maybe he had turned back, or fallen, she didn't care. She shuffled forward along the ruined bridge. The rocks and skirt of land were rising up to meet the metal platform, green bushes underneath, greenblue. Zach paused, then turned round and walked off the end of the viaduct, elegantly, as if dismounting a tightrope. Becca let go of the rail, half-stepped and half-dropped onto the rocky path and knelt. Her whole body was trembling, the tension dropping out in soft tresses. She wanted to cry properly, to curl up and howl. On the ground, the tiny orange flowers shuddered. How quickly death could pass over, and then it wasn't believable anymore. She looked up at Zach. He was facing the other way, looking down the coast and drawing the reefer tin out of his pocket, Zachary again. She'd only known him two days.

Behind them, she could hear Joe cursing, calling Zach a boknaaier, saying that was the last time ever, ever he was going to cross Kaaimans and they could go back along the roadway even if it took two hours longer.

You all right, Becs? he asked. Saying a prayer down there?

She's fine, man, let's just have a moment, said Zach.

Good. I need one. Where's the fokken dagga?

Becca sat at the side of the tracks and looked back at the viaduct. It curved across the estuary in a grizzled, rusty bow. It wasn't that high, not as high as the cliffs at Whitby. The tracks disappeared round the headland. The sea rolled in, from far out, from someplace colder than she could imagine. A song began playing in her head.

Mr Sandman, bring me a dream . . .

· Luxury Hour ·

It was the last week of the season and the lido was nearly deserted. She arrived at the usual time, changed into her suit, left her clothes in a locker and walked out across the chlorine-scented vault. The concrete paving had traces of frost in the corners and was almost painful on the soles of her feet. Light rustled under the blue surface. She climbed down the metal ladder and moved away from the edge without pausing. In October, entering the unheated pool was an act of bravery; she had to remain thoughtless. The water was coldly radiant. Her limbs felt stiff as she kicked and her chin burned. At the halfway mark she looked up at the guard, who was sinking into the fur hood of his parka. Nothing in his demeanour gave the impression of a man ready to intervene, should it be necessary. She took a breath and put her head underwater, surfacing a few strokes later. She was awake now, her heart jabbing. She turned onto her back, rotated her arms, kicked hard. The clouds above were grey and fast. Rain later, perhaps.

She swam twenty lengths, then rested her head on

the coping and caught her breath. The pool slopped gently against her chest. Light filaments flashed and extinguished in the rocking fluid. In summer it was impossible to swim, there was no space; the pool was choppy, kids bombed in at the deep end. Barely an inch between sunbathers. Not many came after early September. But the old couple with rubber caps she always saw in the morning were in the next lane, swimming side by side: her chin tipped high, his submerged. She followed in their wake. They nodded hello when she reached the deep end, and she smiled. She climbed out. Her breasts and thighs were blotched red with the chill and exertion.

In the changing room she tried not to look at her midriff in the mirrors, the crêping and the collapse. She showered and dressed, and went into the poolside cafe. It was busy as usual. There were prams parked between tables, people working on laptops and reading books. The debris of muesli, pastries and napkins was strewn about. On the walls were photographs from the thirties, pictures of young women diving from the high board – now dismantled – or posing with their hands on their hips. The grace, the vivacity, of another era: dark, lipsticked mouths, straight teeth, a kind of ebullient confidence. Their bikinis were high-waisted and scalloped. The scenes looked pre-industrial – open sky, a quality of light. The five-storey civic building opposite the park hadn't been built. London had not yet encroached.

The man behind the counter leaned away from the growling espresso machine and predicted her order.

Latte?

Please.

There was an immaculate row of silver rings in his bottom lip. His head was shaved in a striped pattern.

Bring it over.

She took a seat by the window, in the corner, and watched the old couple emerge from the lido. Their stamina was far greater than hers – an hour's swimming at least. They stood dripping and chatting for a moment as if unaffected by the smart breeze. The woman's legs were strung with thin muscles. Her belly was a tiny mound under the swimming costume. The man had a buckled torso, a white beard. There was a vast laparotomy scar up his abdomen. They were the same height and seemed perfectly suited, even their red caps matched. She wondered if they'd evolved towards their symmetry over the years. Had they ever fought and lied? Had they slammed doors or posted secret letters? The couple parted and went towards separate changing rooms. He walked awkwardly, favouring one hip. In the pool he swam well. Occasionally she'd seen his sedate, companionable breaststroke morph into an energetic butterfly.

There was no one left in the lido. The guard rested his head on his hand, eyes closed, the whistle attached to his wrist hung in the air. The surface of the pool stilled to a beautiful chemical blue.

Her coffee arrived. She opened a packet of sugar. She shouldn't be taking sugar – the baby weight was still not coming off – but she hadn't ever been able to drink coffee without. She sipped slowly. The pool was hypnotic; something about the water was calming, rapturous almost. Time here, after swimming, always felt inadmissible to her day. She would linger, ignore her phone. Often she had to race round the shops to be back in time for the sitter. *Luxury hour*, Daniel called it, as if she was indulging herself, but it was the only time she had without the baby.

After a while she went to the counter, paid, and left. She began to walk home through the park. The breeze was strengthening, the leaves of the trees moving briskly. There were some kids playing cycle polo on one of the hard courts, wheeling about and whacking the puck against the metal cage. Dogs bounded across the grass. She passed the glass-merchant's mansion and the old glassworks, both hidden under flapping plastic drapes and renovation scaffolding. The buildings were being converted into a gallery and she'd begun to wonder about applying for a job.

She'd hated the city when she and Daniel had first

arrived. She'd missed the Devon countryside, the fragrance of peat and gorse, horses with torn manes, the lack of people. But it was what one did, for the better-paid jobs, for the culture; London's sacrificial gravity was too strong. She'd hated the filth, the industrial claustrophobia, immoral rents. Discovering the park had changed everything, and the nearby property was, just about, affordable – two-bedroom flats carved out of the modest houses of nineteenth-century artisans.

She passed through a rank of dark-trunked sycamores. Beyond was the meadow. Its pale brindle stirred in the wind, belts of grass lightening and darkening. The field had been resown after a local campaign by the Friends of the Park – she'd signed their petition. For a century it had been a wasteland. The horses used to pull the carts of quartz sand to the glassworks had over-grazed it. Dust, cullet, and oil from the annealing ovens had polluted the soil. Now it was lush again, there were bees and mice, even city kestrels – she'd seen them tremoring above the burrows, stooping with astonishing speed. It almost reminded her of home. What did people do without access to such places, places less governed, she wondered. Turn to stone.

There was a dry, chaff-like smell to the meadow; the grasses clicked and hushed. The enormous, elaborate spider webs of the previous month had broken apart and were drifting free. A man was walking down the scythed path towards her. She stepped aside to let him pass but he stopped and held out his hand.

Emma?

She looked up. For a second she didn't recognize him. He had on a tie and a suit jacket. The planes of his face came into focus. The heavy bones, the irises with their strange uniformity of colour, no divisions or rings. He was a little older, his hair darker than she remembered, but it was him.

Oh, God, she said. Hi.

He moved to kiss her cheek. She put a hand on his arm, turned her face too much and he kissed her ear, awkwardly.

Do you still live around here?

Yes, I'm over on Hillworth. Near the station.

Nice area.

Yes, she said. It is nice.

The wind was throwing her hair around her face. She hadn't properly washed or brushed the tangles in the changing room. She moved a damp strand from her forehead. It felt sticky with chlorine. He was looking at her, his expression unreadable.

I've been swimming, she explained.

At the lido?

She nodded.

Wow! It's still open? I should go there. Is it cold?

It's OK. Bracing.

Had he forgotten? The cold water never used to bother him. She ran a hand through her hair again, tried to think what to say. Her mind felt white, soft. The shock of the real. Even though he'd said he was leaving, she'd expected to run into him and had, for a time, avoided the area. After a few months the expectation had lessened, and the hope. Then the baby had come, and life had altered drastically. She'd assumed he'd moved away for good. His face was becoming increasingly familiar the more she looked. The shape of his mouth, too full, too voluptuous for a man, the fine white scar in the upper lip.

So, where are you these days? she asked.

Brighton.

Brighton!

I know!

He smiled. One of his front teeth was a fraction squarer, made of porcelain – the accident on his bike while at medical school, she could recall the story. She'd liked tapping it, then the tooth next to it, to hear the difference. Heat bloomed up her neck. These days she could not remember anything – where her purse was, which breast she had last fed the baby on, the name of the artist from her university dissertation. But she could remember his mouth, and lying so close to his face that its structure began to blur. She felt as if she might reach out now and touch the hard wet surface of his broken tooth. She put her hands in her coat pockets. Around them the grass was swaying and hissing. A bird darted out of the field, flew a few feet and then disappeared between stalks.

He was studying her too. Probably she looked tired, leached, and aged, the classic new mother's demeanour, not like the woman who had come up to him in a low-cut swimsuit and asked to borrow change for the locker.

I'll pay you back tomorrow.

I might not be here tomorrow.

Yes, you will.

So confident, then.

She hadn't applied makeup, there was no point most days really, and her mouth was dry and bitter from the coffee. At least the long coat hid her figure. There was no point avoiding the obvious question.

Did you go to Burma? she asked.

Myanmar, he corrected, quietly. I did. Well, officially to Thailand, but we went across the border most days into the training camps.

I thought you would.

Now it's not such a problem getting in. Tourism.

She nodded. She was not up to speed on such things anymore.

Was it difficult?

She wasn't sure what she meant by this question,

only that she imagined privation, forfeit, that he had made the wrong decision.

Sometimes. We had a decent team. A lot of them were more missionaries than doctors really, but on the whole the quality was good. I don't know whether we helped. The students qualified, then got arrested for practising.

He shrugged. He glanced towards the north end of the park.

So it's still open?

Yes. Last week before winter closing. You should go before it shuts.

For old time's sake. She did not say it. Nor, *why have you come back?*

He glanced at his watch.

I have a conference. I'm presenting the first paper, actually. I have to get to Barts.

Oh. Congratulations.

He had obviously come up the ranks. Hence the suit, the tidy version of his former self. He shrugged again. Humility, but the duty was clearly very important. There was a pause. She could barely look at him; the past was restoring itself too viscerally. Since the baby she had felt nothing, no desire, not even sorrow that this part of her life seemed to have vanished, perhaps for good. Daniel had been understanding, of course, patient. She couldn't explain it; breastfeeding, different priorities, the wrong smell, and when she looked at the baby she felt redefined. Now, there was a familiar low ache. She wanted to step forward, reach out. *Compatible immune systems*, he had once said, to explain their impulses, the heedless attraction, *that's all it really is. That's all*, she'd asked?

For something to do she took her bag off her shoulder and rummaged around inside. It was a pointless act, spurred by panic. But then, in the inside pocket, she found the season ticket. She held it out.

Here. It still has a couple of swims left. They won't check the name when they stamp it, they never do.

He took the pass.

You should go, since you're here.

That's really thoughtful of you, Emma. God, I do miss it!

But you've got the sea? In Brighton?

Yes.

He was grinning now, and she could see in him that uninhibited man who'd never cared about the cold, who'd plunged into the pool without hesitation and swum almost a length under the surface. She could see his damp body on the bed in his flat, the chaos of sheets around them, his expression, agonized, abandoned, as if in a seizure dream. She could see herself, holding the railings of the bed, fighting for control of the space they were using. Walking quickly home, ashamed, electrified, holding her swimsuit under the kitchen tap so that it would look used. Luxury hour.

So. What's your life like now? Are you still at the Tate?

No. I'm married.

Ah.

She glanced at him, then looked away.

To Daniel?

Yes, to Daniel.

Any children?

There was nothing to his tone, other than polite conversation, the logical assumption that one thing would follow another. Perhaps a slight wistfulness, some regressive emotion, it was always so hard to tell. The wind moved across the meadow. The grass rippled, like dry water.

No. No children.

As if it could be as it was before. He nodded, neither surprised nor sympathetic. It was suddenly hard for her to breathe, though there were acres of air above them. The lie was so great there would surely be some penalty. She would go home and the house would be silent, her son's room empty, the walls painted white again. Or the baby would be screaming in the cot, and he would smear to ash when she lifted him up. He would be lying motionless in the bath while the minder sat on a stool, wings unfurled, monstrous.

Her old lover was speaking, saying something about his engagement to a woman from Thailand; her name was Sook, his family liked her, they had no children yet either. He was holding the season pass. He looked contented, established, a man in a tie about to give an important paper. Everything had moved on, except that he was here, and this was not the way to Barts. She reached out and touched his arm. He was real, of course he was.

You should swim, she said. Will you swim?

He looked at his watch again.

Yeah. Why not. I reckon there's time, if I'm quick. What shall I wear? Will I get away with boxers?

I have to go, she said.

Oh. OK.

It was too abrupt, she knew, a breach in the otherwise civil conversation that should have wound up more carefully. But already she had turned and was walking away up the path, the wind cold in her hair. His voice, calling behind her.

Bye, Emma. Lovely seeing you again.

She kept walking. She did not turn round. At the edge of the meadow she stepped off the track, put her bag down, and crouched in the grass. He would not follow her, she knew, but she stayed there a long time, hidden. From her bag came the faint sound of ringing. She was late for the sitter. She stayed crouched, stupidly, until her legs felt stiff. In the earth, between stalks, were tiny pieces of brown glass from the old works. Enormous hurrying clouds above, but the rain was still holding off.

Eventually, she stood and looked back. He was gone. If she ran to the lido maybe she could catch him. She could apologize, and explain everything, tell him that she'd been afraid, she'd been angry and hurt that he was leaving; she'd had to choose, like he'd had to choose. The baby was a complication, but she could tell him what the child's name was at least, if nothing else, he should know that. They could exchange phone numbers. They could meet, somewhere between Brighton and here. Or she could just watch him through the cafe window, from the corner table, a woman from the past. She could watch him swim, his body a long shadow under the surface.

· Later, His Ghost ·

The wind was coming from the east when he woke. The windows on that side of the house boxed and clattered in their frames, even behind the stormboards, and the corrugated-iron sheet over the coop in the garden was hawing and creaking, as though it might rip out of its rivets and fly off. The bellowing had come into his sleep, like a man's voice. December 23rd. The morning was dark, or it was still night, the clock was dead. He lay unmoving beneath the blankets, his feet cold in his boots, chest sore from breathing unheated air. The fire had gone out; the wood had burned too high again with the pull up the chimney. It was hard keeping it in overnight. Coal was much better; it burned longer, but was hard to find and too heavy to carry.

He pulled the blankets over his face. *Get up*, he thought. If he didn't get up it would be the beginning of the end. People who stayed inside got into trouble. No one helped them. Part of him understood – who wanted to die outside, tossed about like a piece of litter, stripped of clothing by the wind and lodged somewhere, dirt blowing dunes over your corpse? Crawling into a calm little shelter was preferable. He understood.

Something hard clattered along the roof, scuttled over the slates, and was borne away. There was a great *oom*ing sound above, almost oceanic, like the top of the sky was heaving and breaking. Whatever had been kept in check by the gulfstream was now able to push back and lash around. People had once created aerial gods, he knew, fiends of the air or the mountaintops. He took it personally, sometimes – yelling uselessly up the chimney, or even into the wind's face, his voice tiny and whipped away. Not often though, because it didn't really help, and the chances of getting hit were worse.

When it came from the east a lot of the remaining house roofs went, and whole walls could topple – another reason not to stay inside too much, you had to be alert to the collapses. But this house was good; it had survived. He turned on his side and shivered as the cold crept down his neck. The sofa he was lying on always felt damp. The cushion he was using as a pillow smelled of wet mortar. He didn't usually sleep in this room, but Helene was now in his. He would have liked them to sleep together, to be warmer.

Another object crashed past the house, splintering against the gable, and flying off in separate clattering pieces. He couldn't remember the last still day, the trees standing upright and placid. Stillness seemed like a childhood myth, like August hay-timing, or Father Christmas. Last night, he'd slept restlessly; his dreams were turbulent – wars, animals stampeding, and Craig, always Craig. After a night like that it was hard to get going.

Get up, he thought. And then, because it was too difficult today, he thought, *Buffalo*. He pictured a buffalo. It was enormous and black-brown. It had a giant head and the shoulders of a weightlifter, a tapered back end, small, upturned horns. The image came from a picture he'd kept in a box in the bunker, one of the things Craig had taken. The buffalo looked permanently, structurally braced.

He sat up, moved the blankets away, and stood. He found the torch next to the sofa and switched it on. The cold made him feel old and stiff. He moved around and lifted his legs gymnastically to get his blood moving. He did some lunges, like warming up for football. There was a portable gas stove in the corner of the room and he set the torch next to it, ignited the ring, boiled a cup of water and made tea. He drank the tea black. He missed milk most of all. There weren't even any smuts in the grate. Perhaps he'd leave the fire a day to save fuel – the temperature was about four or five degrees, he guessed, manageable. So long as Helene was warm enough.

He took the torch and moved through the building to the room where she slept. It was warmish. Her fire was still glowing orange. She slept with the little Tilley lamp on. She didn't like the dark. She was sound asleep, lying on her side, her belly vast under her jumper. He picked up one of the blankets from the floor and put it back over her. She didn't move. She seemed peaceful, though her eyes were moving rapidly behind her eyelids. The wind was quieter this side of the house, leeside. It whistled and whined and slipstreamed away. Little skitters of soot came down the chimney and sparks rose from the cradle. He looked at Helene sleeping. Her hair was cut short, like his, but hers curled and was black. When they were open her eyes were extremely pretty. A lot of the boys in school had fancied her. He imagined climbing onto the bed and putting his arm over her shoulder. Sometimes when he was checking on her she woke up and looked at him. Mostly she knew he was just checking, bringing her tea, or some food, or more wood for the fire. But sometimes she panicked. And he knew she was worried about the baby coming; that frightened him too. He'd found a medical book on one of his explorations, but still.

She'd done well, he thought, lasting it out, but she was very quiet, mostly. He thought probably she hadn't developed any methods to help, like picturing the buffalo. She was probably thirty, or thirty-five. She'd been an English teacher, though not his; she hadn't recognized him when he'd found her. She liked sardines in tomato sauce, which was good because he had lots of tins. She always thanked him for the food. *That's all right*, he'd say, and sometimes he'd almost add, *Miss McDowell*. She never said anything about what had happened to her, or the baby, but he could guess. No one would choose that now. He'd found her in the Catholic cathedral, what was left of it. There were two dead bodies nearby, both men; they looked freshly dead, with a lot of blood. She was looking up at the circular hole where the rose window had been. She wasn't praying or crying. He thought she'd done well.

He left tea for her in a metal cup with a lid, and some sardines, and went back to his room. He did a stock check. He did this every day, unnecessarily, but it made him feel calmer. Calor gas bottles, food, clothes, batteries (one less for the dead clock), duct tape, painkillers, knives, rope. The cans were piled in such a way that he could count them by tens. This house still had water, a slow trickling stream that was often tinted and tasted earthy. He still hadn't worked out if the property had its own well, lots of the garden was buried. But it made life easier – he didn't have to rig up a rainwater funnel. He'd been collecting packets of baby formula too, but when he'd showed

Helene she'd looked confused, then sad. There was a box with more delicate things inside, frivolous things, photographs – of his mother, and his little brother in school uniform – his passport, though that was useless now other than to prove who he was, and the pages he'd been collecting for Helene. There wasn't much to read in the house. He'd been hunting for the play for a month or two and it was a very difficult task, most books had been destroyed, the wind was an expert at that. Once buildings were breached, nothing paper lasted; it warped and pulped, the ink smudged. Sometimes he found just a paragraph, or a line, on an otherwise unreadable page.

So dear the love my people bore me, nor set a mark so bloody on the business: but with fairer colours painted their foul ends. In few, they hurried us aboard a bark, bore us some leagues to sea, where they'd prepared a rotten carcass of a boat, not rigg'd . . .

The town's library had been demolished in the first big storms. No wonder: it had been built in the sixties, as part of the civic centre. The older the building, the longer it lasted, generally: people had gotten very bad at construction, he thought, or lazy. He was very good at salvaging now. He was good at it because he was good at moving around outside. He wasn't timid, but he never took anything for granted either. He wore the rucksack strapped tight to his body, like a parachute.

He taped up his arms and legs so they wouldn't billow, he tested the ropes, and he always looked in every direction for airborne debris. He never, never assumed it was safe. He'd seen too many bodies with blunted heads.

After the stock check, he took a tin of salmon out of the stack, opened it and ate it cold. He was hungry and he ate too fast. His mouth hurt. Ulcers starred his tongue. He probably needed some fruit, but he'd rather give the fruit to Helene. In winter having two meals was important – breakfast and dinner – even if they were small. Otherwise he'd get sick. This was the fourth winter. Last Christmas he hadn't really celebrated because he was by himself, but having Helene made things nicer. He scraped the last flakes out of the tin with his nail and ate them, then drank the oil, which made him gag. He saved the tin – while they were still greasy they were good for making flour-and-water dumplings over the fire, though the dumplings tasted fishy. As well as the surprise gift, he'd been planning their Christmas meal. He'd had a tin of smoked pheasant pâté for two years, it was too special to eat by himself. There was a jar of redcurrant. A jar of boiled potatoes. And a tin of actual Christmas pudding. They would have it all warmed up. Two courses! He even had a miniature whisky, with which to set fire to the pudding. It was important to try to celebrate.

He went to the back of the house, peered through a gap in the stormboards and watched the dawn struggling to arrive. Daylight usually meant the wind eased slightly, but not today. The clouds were fast and the light pulsed, murky yellow aurorae. The usual items sped past on the current – rags, bits of tree, transmuted unknowable things. Sometimes he was amazed there were enough objects left to loosen and scatter. Sometimes he wondered whether these things were just the same million shoes and bottles and cartons, circling the globe endlessly. The clouds passed fat and fast overhead, and were sucked into a vortex on the horizon, disappearing into nothing. There was sleetish rain, travelling horizontally, almost too quickly to see.

It was probably a bad idea to go out today. His rule was nothing more than a ninety, what he gauged to be a ninety. This was worse. But he had two days left and he wanted to find more pages.

He went back to his room and got ready. He put on waterproof trousers and a jacket. He cleaned and put on the goggles. He pulled the hood of the jacket up, yanked the toggles and tied them tightly, a double knot. He taped the neck. He taped his cuffs and his ankles, his knees and his elbows. He put on gloves but left them untaped so he could take them off if he found any more books; he would need his fingers to be nimble, to flick through and tear out. It might mean he would lose a glove, or both, but he'd risk it. When he was done he felt airtight, like some kind of diver, *a storm-diver,* he thought. But it was better not to get heroic. For a while when he'd gone out he'd worn a helmet, but it'd made him feel too bulky, too heavy, not adapted. He weighted the rucksack down with the red stone – he didn't like to think of it as his lucky stone, because he wasn't superstitious, but secretly he did think it was lucky. It was egg-shaped, banded with pink and white – some kind of polished gneiss. He'd found it looking through the wreckage of the geology lab at school. It sat in the bottom of the rucksack, as a ballast, leaving enough room for anything he discovered on his excursions, but preventing the bag's flapping. He had plastic wrapping for anything delicate. He was good at discerning what was useful and what was not; he hadn't brought back many useless things, though the temptation was to save beautiful items, or money. His mother had always joked his birthdays were easy – as a kid he didn't need many toys or field comforts or gadgets. His mother had died of sickness. So had his little brother. So had thousands of other people. It wasn't just the conditions, it was what the conditions led to, Craig had told him. In some ways Craig had been clever.

There were two doors to the house – one on the north side and one on the west. He stood by the west door and thought, *Buffalo.* He opened the door and felt the draw of air, then opened it wider and moved into the alcove behind the storm door. The storm door opened inwards and could be locked either side. He moved the bolt, forced himself out into the buffeting air, planted his feet and fastened the door behind him. Either side of the house, the wind tore past, conveying junk, going about its daily demolition. Behind him, the house felt solid. It was a squat, single-storey longbarn in the low-lying outskirts of town, with shutters and big outer doors. He'd modified it a bit, with nails and planks, building break-walls. This was his fifteenth house. The first – his mother's, a white 1930s semi – had gone down as easily as straw, along with the rest of the row. They'd gone to the gymnasium as part of the reorganization, then to a shared terrace. The brick terraces had proved more durable, he'd lived in two, but they were high-ceilinged; once the big windows and roofs gave out they were easy for the wind to dismantle. Before the barn, he'd been in the bunker near the market with Craig, a sort of utility storage. It was a horrible, rat-like existence – dark, desperate, scavenging. Craig was much older than him. He'd wanted things and had taken things. There had been three big fights, and the last one made such a mess. But he wasn't sorry. Maybe he should have stayed in the bunker alone but he didn't want to. A lighthouse would have been best, round, aerodynamic, deep-sunk into rock, made to withstand batterings. But the coast was impossible. Before everything had gone down he'd seen news footage; he couldn't quite believe the towering swells, the surges. He had nightmares about those waves reaching this far inland.

He inched along the barn wall, towards the open. He'd planned a new route through town. He would keep to the west side of streets wherever he could, for protection, but that meant being in the path of anything collapsing. In the past he'd outrun avalanching walls, he'd been picked up and flung against hard surfaces and rubble heaps, his collarbone and his wrist had been fractured. There were only so many near misses. He would need to judge the soundness of structures, only venture inside a building if the risks seemed low. He would go into the Golden Triangle – some of the big Victorian houses there were still holding and they were more likely to have what he was looking for. At the corner of the barn he knelt, tensed his neck and shoulder muscles and put his head out into the rushing wind. The force was immense. He checked for large oncoming objects, then began to crawl along the ground. What had once been the longbarn's garden was now stripped bald of grass and the walls were in heaps. Clods of earth tumbled past him. The wind shunted his backside and slid him forward. He flattened out and moved like a lizard towards the farm buildings and the first rope. He had different techniques, depending on the situation. Sometimes he crawled miles and came back bruised black underneath. Sometimes he crouched like an ape and lumbered. Other times he made dashes, if there were intermittent blasts, cannonballing the lulls, but he could get caught out doing that. Sometimes it was better to walk into the wind head on, sometimes leaning back against it and digging your heels in worked.

It'd been a while since he'd been out in anything this strong. It was terrifying and exhilarating. The wind bent him over when he tried to stand, so he stayed low, a creature of stealth and avoidance. He clung to the cord that ran between the buildings. He'd rigged it himself and had tested the binding only a few days ago, but still he gave a good yank to make sure it hadn't begun to untether. A lot of the ones in town he'd redone too. He traversed slowly while the wind bore between the buildings. After the farm, there was a dangerous open stretch. The Huff, he called it, because the weather always seemed in a filthy temper there. It had been a racecourse, quite famous. Beyond it, the town started properly: its suburbs, its alleys and piles of stone. Once it had been a town of magnificent trees. Plane trees, beeches, oaks: the big avenues had been lined by them, their leaves on fire in autumn, raining blossom in spring. Now they were mostly gone – uprooted and dying. There was a lot of firewood to haul away. He hardly ever saw anyone else taking it. He could probably count on one hand the number of people he saw in a month. Occasionally, a big armoured vehicle passed through, military – its windows covered in metal grilles. The soldiers never got out. A lot of people had gone to towns in the west because it was supposed to be milder, there was supposed to be more protection. He didn't believe that really.

When he got to the Huff he almost changed his mind and went back. The air above was thick with dirt, a great sweeping cloud of it. There was a constant howling. Every few moments something rattled, fluttered or spun past, bounced off the ground and was lobbed upwards. On tamer days he'd sledged across the stretch on a big metal tray, for fun, putting his heels down to slow the contraption and flinging himself sideways to get off. Today, no larks, he'd be lucky not to break his neck. It was too wide a tract of land to rope; he had to go without moorings. Crossing would mean surrendering to the wind, becoming one of many hurled items, colliding with others, abraded, like a pellet in a shaker.

He gave himself a moment or two to prepare and then he let go of the farm walls and began to crawl across. He tried to move quickly to keep up with the thrust of the current, but it was too strong. Within moments the wind had taken him, lifting his back end and tossing him over. He felt the red stone slam into his spine. He started tobogganing, feet first. He tucked his head in, rolled on his side, brought his knees up. The ground was hard and bumpy and pounded his bones. He put his hands down and felt debris filling his cuffs. Something sharp caught his ankle bone and stung. *Shit*, he thought, *shitshitshit.* But he went with it, there was nothing he could do, and after a second or two he managed to regain some control. He hoofed his boots down and tried to brake. He was nearly at the edge of the racecourse, where the old, flint wall of the town began. The wind shoved him hard again and he went tumbling forward. He presented his back and hit the pointed stones and stopped.

He lay for a moment, dazed, brunted against the structure, with dirt pattering around him. It was hard to breathe. The air tasted of soil. He turned his head, and spat. When he opened his eyes one pane of the goggles was cracked, splitting his view. His ankle throbbed. Other than that he was all right, but he had to get moving. He pushed himself up and crawled along the boundary wall, around trolleys and piles of swept rubbish. At the first gap he went through. He sat up, leant against the flints and caught his breath while the wind roared the other side.

He bent and flexed his leg, cleaned his goggles,

emptied his gloves. *Moron*, he thought. He did want to live, moments like this reminded him. He sat for a time, tried to relax. The boundary wall was twelve feet thick and sturdy. Whoever had built it had meant business. Probably the Romans. Sections along the river had been restored when he was a kid, as part of the 'fan-Tas-tic flood defence initiative'.

He looked at the town. Roofs and upper floors were gone; cars were parked on their backs, their windscreens smashed. The big storms had left domino rubble in every direction, scattered fans of bricks and tiles, bouquets of splintered wood. Old maps meant nothing, new streets had been made, buildings rearranged. He had to keep relearning its form as its composition shifted.

He got up, crouched low, surveyed the route and limped off. It was a mile to the Golden Triangle, through Tombland and the market. He saw no one. He kept to the safer routes and used the secure ropes when he had to, hauling himself along. He squinted through the broken goggles, seeing an odd spider-like creature everywhere in front of him, but he didn't take them off – the last thing he needed was to be blinded. The ruins were depressing, but he occasionally saw miraculous things in them. An animal, though they were rare. There were no birds, not even distressed gulls; nothing could cope in the torrent. The rats had done OK, anything living below ground level. Cats and dogs were few, always emaciated and wretched. There was no food, nothing growing, and not much to kill. People's survival instincts were far worse, he often thought, but they could at least use can openers. Two years ago, on the edge of the Huff, he'd seen a stag, a fantastic thing. It was reddish, six points on each antler, standing perfectly still, like something from the middle of a forest, as if it had always stood there, as if tree after tree had been stripped away, until the forest was gone and there was nothing left to shield it. He'd seen awful things too. A man sliced in half by a flying glass pane, his entrails worming from his stomach. Craig's broken skull, the soft, foul matter inside. Who you became afterwards was who you told yourself you were. Good things had to be held onto, and remembered, and celebrated. That was why he had to get the pages for Helene and why they would try to have a nice Christmas.

He made his way slowly through the town, forcing his body against the blast, starting to favour one leg as his ankle stiffened. He kept leeside wherever he could and watched for flying timber and rockslides. He crossed the little park at the edge of the Golden Triangle. There were stumps where the central pavilion had stood. The trees lying on the ground were scoured bare. Sleet had begun to gather along their trunks. He hoped it wouldn't turn to snow; it was hard enough keeping his footing.

When he got to the district he was surprised to see smoke leaking from one of the heaps. He made his way over, cautiously, but it was just a random fire burning along a beam, some stray electrical spark perhaps, or friction. Two rows away the houses were in better shape, some only had holes in the roofs and lopped-off chimneys. The windows were mostly gone. He could hop through the bays if the lintels were safe. He always called out to make sure they were empty first. He'd been in some of the houses before, checking for food, batteries, essentials. They'd been lovely places once, owned by doctors and lawyers, he imagined – his mum had always wanted to live there. There were remnants of cast-iron fireplaces, painted tiles; even some crescents of stained glass hanging on above the doorframes. He tried a couple, searching through the downstairs rooms – he never went upstairs if he could help it, it was too dangerous. The wind moaned through the rooms, shifting wet curtains and making the peeling wallpaper flicker. Damp and lichen speckled the walls and fungus grew from the skirting boards. There were pulpy masses on the shelves, rotting covers, the sour smell of macerating paper. He stepped among the detritus, broken glass and broken furniture, digging through piles, tossing collapsed volumes aside like wet mushrooms. He'd been dreaming about finding a complete works since he'd found Helene – that would really be something special – bound in plastic perhaps, unviolated. But, like Bibles, they were the first to go, their pages wafer thin, like ghost's breath. He'd studied the play in school, not with any particular enjoyment, he'd been better at science. He could remember bits of it, the parts he'd had to read out. *As wicked dew as e'er my mother brush'd with raven's feather from unwholesome fen drop on you both! A south-west blow on ye . . .* He was sure Helene had taught it; certainly she'd have read it. Reading it again might help her. She could begin to think differently. She could read it while she fed the baby. So far she'd said nothing about the baby, not even any names she liked. Sometimes she put her hand on her stomach, when the baby was moving. He'd found some sections of the play, dried the pages, sorted the scenes and put them in order, as best he could. He'd glued and glued things in between. It wasn't an attractive-looking gift; he'd never been very artistic.

After ten or eleven houses he was starting to lose hope and was worried about the daylight. The wind was not letting up: if anything it was gaining power. There'd been a couple of worryingly big bangs nearby, something shattering, a frenzied thudding. He went back out onto the street. There was a big house further along, free-standing, walled. It had upper bays as well as lower. A vicarage, maybe. Part of the roof was gone. The gate was padlocked but the frame had come away from the post and he forced his way through the gap. In the garden the plant pots and urns were smashed apart but a small fruit tree was still standing, defiantly, petrified black globes hanging in its branches. He checked round the periphery of the house. Then he went through a lower window and down a hallway. His ankle felt sore, but that was OK, injuries you couldn't feel were far worse.

He knew, even before he got to the big room at the back of the house, that he was going to find what he was looking for. Some things you knew, like echoes, good and bad things that were about to happen. He forced a swollen door into a parlour. It was quite quiet inside, not too much damage or decay. It would have been a nice place to sit and watch TV or read. The walls had once been red but were now darker, browny, like dried blood. There was a fireplace, heaped full of charred wood, pieces of chimney brick and sleeving. There was a man in a chair, a corpse. His eyelids were shrinking upwards over the empty sockets; some wisps of hair left on his head. The skin was yellow and tight and shedding off the cheekbones. A blanket was wrapped around his shoulders, as if he was cold. There was no bad smell in the room, it had happened a long time ago. Probably he had done it himself, a lot of people had. He didn't look too closely at the man. He went over to the shelves. There were rows and rows of hardbacks. He could even read the titles on some of the spines. *Encyclopaedia Britannica. Audubon.* And there was a collection of Shakespeares, mottled, green mould blooming along them, but readable. He found it in the middle. He took off his gloves and opened it carefully; the edges of the paper were moist, stuck, and they tore slightly when moved, but the book held together. He turned gently to the end. *I'll deliver all; and promise you calm seas, auspicious gales and sail so expeditious that shall catch your royal fleet far off.*

He took off his rucksack, wrapped the book in plastic and put it inside one of the small compartments. He put the rucksack back on, clicked the straps across his chest, drew them tight, and put on his gloves. It would be a good house to go through for other things, but he didn't want to get caught out and not be able to get across town and over the Huff to the longbarn. He didn't want to leave Helene alone longer than he had to. He would come back, after Christmas, and search properly. He closed the door on the dead man.

On the way out he saw his own reflection in the dusty, cracked hall mirror. Like books, not many mirrors were left either, the wind loved killing them. Probably a good thing. His coat hood was drawn tightly around his head; he was earless and bug-eyed, and one eye lens was shattered. The metallic tape around his neck shone like scales. He looked like some kind of demon. Maybe that's what he was, maybe that's what he'd become. But he felt human; he remembered feeling human. His ankle hurt, which was good. He could use a can opener. And he liked Christmas. He turned away from the mirror and climbed back out of the window. Snow was flying past.

· Goodnight Nobody ·

Jem had seen the dog the week before, the day after her birthday, while she'd been breaking in her new shoes. It was a small dog, a Jack Russell or a terrier, not something that looked dangerous like the muscley Doberman and the mint-eyed Alsatian further down the street. She'd seen the man walking the dog by the weir, and she'd seen it tied up outside the Saracen's Head. It didn't choke its lead or drool or go for people. The man was hard-faced though, hair buzzed to the scalp, tight jeans he was too old to wear, dark red boots laced up his shins. He had a tattoo on his neck. A web. Or a net. Something stringy. Mumm-Ra said tattoos outside the collar and cuff meant people were beyond civilization. Mumm-Ra saw a lot of tattoos at work, in all kinds of hidden places. She often told Gran about them. Once a woman with only one breast had had one where the other breast wasn't. A rose.

Outside the man's house there was a police van. It'd been there all morning. The lights and the engine were off, but it was very noticeable, very nosey-looking. They would be taking the dog away soon, Jem was sure. The kids on the street had been trying to climb the back-yard wall for a look-see before it was destroyed, even though it was the same dog it'd been the week before, nothing extra special or with superpowers.

Destroyed made the dog sound like a battleship in a war game. Jem wondered how they'd do it – a gun, maybe, or by injection, like criminals in America. The dog would twitch and go to sleep and then its heart would stop. They'd been learning about the heart in biology. The heart was the last piece of equipment to keep going in a body; it worked the hardest. One cell told all the others what to do, and if the main cell died another normal cell took over. She'd shared that piece of information with Mumm-Ra and Gran. Gran had said it sounded like socialism. Dictatorship, more like, Mumm-Ra said. A vet might come to the man's house and put the dog down, the same as if the dog had cancer or a broken leg. The dog wouldn't know what was happening, so it wouldn't be scared, although dogs did understand, they could sense things.

Martin, Jem's dad, had had cancer. He was extremely lucky. He had one lung and he'd had chemotherapy while living in his caravan in Catton Park. It'd taken months for him to get better and during that time Jem hadn't seen him much. He'd said, before he'd been told he would be fine, that if he wasn't going to be fine he wanted to be put down. Before he started to mess himself. He wanted sleeping pills or to be dropped off the bridge into the river. After the chemotherapy Martin's eyebrows didn't come back.

He still smoked sometimes, at the pub, and after tea. Mumm-Ra said he was an imbecile and would be seeing her soon enough if he didn't stop – she'd be zipping him up. Mumm-Ra worked in the mortuary at the hospital. She wore blue scrubs. She looked like a doctor, but she wasn't one, even though she'd taken exams as part of the job. A practical exam and a written exam. After she'd said the thing about Martin, Jem had wondered for a while about people being zipped up, as if they were bags. She knew it meant something else. Jem didn't like to think about what Mumm-Ra did at work, which involved glue and chemicals, and not crying while other people cried.

Mortuary. Mortuary. Sometimes words got stuck in her head, usually if they sounded a certain way – strong, important.

The street had been busy all morning. It wasn't raining. People were standing about with their front doors open and their arms crossed and they were talking about what had happened and waiting to hear more. Before Gran had gone, Jem had been standing around too. The rules about who you could talk to, when, and where, had been suspended. People she didn't know had said things to her like, What a tragedy, and, Oh my

Lord. She'd even missed watching *Thundercats*, which was her favourite programme.

The baby had been a tiny baby, a newborn. No one knew if it was a girl or a boy or what its name was. Maybe it didn't have a name yet. People on the street had seemed angry there was no name and were tutting a lot. She wondered if that meant the baby wasn't a proper person yet, or was beyond civilization.

Jem's brother hadn't seemed like a proper person until he'd been given his name. Mumm-Ra had been too sad to give him a name in the first week because his dad had gone back to Yugoslavia. For good, because of the war. She'd also had a Caesarean so she couldn't come downstairs. Caesarean. Mumm-Ra had a smiley scar that was hidden by the hair there, and a skin fold, not that Jem saw that part much. Gran had had some serious words with Mumm-Ra and then they'd taken Jem's brother to the town hall. Her brother was called Sava. It was a name from his dad's country – Gran had found it in a book. Everyone called him Sav. Jem couldn't really remember Sav's dad, except for his red checked shirt and jars of sweet pickled seafood that he ate on black crackers. Mumm-Ra and Martin had chosen Jem's name together before they'd split up. Jemima. Jem hated it. Posh, or a duck, were the bullying options. Everyone called her Jem, luckily, but that didn't stop people not liking her at school. Mum had become Mumm-Ra after *Thundercats* Series One and the big argument over Jem's bike and because of her job. Jem never said it out loud though. Gran's real name was Marcy. You couldn't write a report at school about a book unless you said why the characters were called what they were and what it meant. Naming humans was complicated, and went wrong really easily, and people fought about it, so Jem hadn't minded if the baby didn't have a name. It was neglect, people were saying, poor little mite.

People were also saying that the baby had been left outside in a basket in the yard, near the kennel. It'd been crying for hours. Dogs didn't like crying babies. The man's girlfriend was very thin and hadn't even looked pregnant. Then she was holding a screechy bundle outside their front door and there was a big party and the next day there were bin-bags full of bottles and cans on the pavement. Jem didn't know their names, the man and his girlfriend. They lived thirty-two doors down. That was very close. If what had happened had been an asteroid, it would have hit Jem's house too, but asteroids were rare and they usually hit deserts.

The baby had already been taken away in an ambulance. The man had been taken away by the police, because he was the dog's owner and responsible. Possibly he was also drunk. Someone who had passed by the house had looked in and said that the girlfriend was sitting at the kitchen table, not crying, just drinking a can of lager. Someone else had said that she was hysterical; she'd screamed and hit the policeman who'd arrested her boyfriend. Hysterical. Jem had thought that meant funny.

It was hard to know what to believe. She didn't have any friends on the street. Deborah Mason lived a few doors down, but she and Deborah were not friends. Deborah called Sav a half-caste commie bastard. She called Jem duck-fuck. She said once that *Thundercats* was a stupid television programme, why did they have blue faces? Jem tried to explain they didn't, only Panthro, and actually his face was grey, which had made things worse. She'd ended up with a horse-pinch on the arm that was red and sore for a week. Deborah was two years older than Jem and at a different school, but they took the same bus. Deborah was always talking about her periods, but she called it red-eye or painters or the-blob, and her Tampax was always in wrong and uncomfortable, and it made the whole thing sound horrible.

Deborah had talked to Jem earlier on the street though, in a normal conversation, without any insults. She'd said the baby had been picked up by the neck and shaken to death. The dog had bitten right through the baby's neck. Decapitated it. Then it had licked up all the blood. Deborah's mouth looked horrible when she said this, glistening and dramatic, and her tongue tip came out between her teeth. Some of what she said might have been true, but a lot definitely wasn't. Jem had nodded and tried to look impressed. You made the most of it when the rules were gone. But after a second or two, Deborah's face had gone blurry, as if she was under a swimming pool. Jem's stomach had sent a bile bubble up to her mouth, which popped and tasted disgusting. Gran had called her in not long after that to mind Sav because she was going to the social club and Mumm-Ra wasn't back from her night shift.

Mumm-Ra was home now, looking withered and baggy in her uniform. She was moving around the kitchen slowly. She was, Jem knew, capable of turning into a monster if everyone wasn't careful. Night shifts were killing her, Gran often said, but Jem knew her mother would never die, just like actual Mumm-Ra, it was impossible. She was far too powerful. There were probably a lot of evil spirits where she worked, which might help summon her strength. Jem didn't really believe in spirits and thought the séances some of the girls in her class had done in the store cupboard were stupid, obviously fake. Night shifts paid well though, especially at weekends.

Mumm-Ra was opening a tin of tomato soup, while Sav flicked bits of baby food all over the floor. Mumm-

Ra had cut her hair very short last year because Sav was a puker and she was sick of washing sick out of it. Other mothers got perms and crimps. From behind, in the uniform, she looked almost like a man.

Sav was nearly two. He was extremely strong and didn't like to do what anyone wanted him to do. He liked to prod eyes and to smash down towers of objects he'd stacked. Steering him along to the newsagent's to get sweets or collect Gran's paper was impossible. If the man's dog had gone for Sav, he probably would have blinded it.

It's not the dog that should be put down, Mumm-Ra was saying, quietly. Some people should have to get a licence to breed. She was up to speed on the situation, even though she'd only just got back. Maybe she'd seen the baby. Maybe she'd actually been handling the baby. Putting it back together. Making it look not so bad for the relatives, with powders and cream. Cosseting, it was called. Gran said what Mumm-Ra did was sort of what a beautician did, but much harder.

Jem never talked about Mumm-Ra's job. If people asked in school, she always said hospital orderly or a nurse. The source of all Mumm-Ra's power probably came from her ability to do what she did to bodies, which didn't scare her, though Gran said it certainly took its toll. Because death, and people's grief, were exhausting. Morticians often had to stop working. Some went mad, really mad, with roaring in their heads, or they disappeared and were found in the woods. Nerves of ice, Martin said about Mumm-Ra.

Martin wasn't able to pay much money towards Jem, some months nothing at all. He did get disability benefit for having only one lung though. And the house they lived in had belonged to Martin's mother. Useless, is what Mumm-Ra said about Martin, a useless lump, but they were quite like friends. Martin had even put his arm around Mumm-Ra when Sav's dad left and had offered to stay. Mumm-Ra said no. No, no, we're the opposite, Martin, the absolute opposite. Sav's dad was a roofer, an expert roofer; he'd worked on the repairs on the prison in the castle. He'd worked legally. Then he'd gone back home because men especially were needed. Unlucky in love, Gran said about Mumm-Ra. She likes the leavers, your mother. If a man won't marry you before the babies come, Jemima, he'll be gone after. That fellow will have a family, I bet, never mind any war.

Gran had bits and bobs of wisdom about men. Her husband had died before Jem was born. He'd been called Leonard. Gran had burgundy hair that was white at the roots. She drove a green Maxi and could fix the fanbelt herself when it squealed. There were always soft mints and a packet of Merits in her purse. She slept in Mumm-Ra's room overnight when Mumm-Ra was working.

Mumm-Ra stirred the tomato soup. Sav put his dinner bowl on his head and orange goo smeared into his hair. Then he flung the bowl at Mumm-Ra and a splattery streak went up the back of her scrubs. Hell's teeth, she said, without turning round. Sort him out will you, Jem. Your gran'll be back soon. But it's Saturday, Jem wanted to say. She didn't say it because Mumm-Ra turned round and gave her a look that involved not blinking and the kitchen light dimmed a bit. Mumm-Ra could sense things coming like a dog could. She took the soup upstairs on a tray.

Jem decided that when Sav was having his after-lunch nap, she'd go out again and see what was happening. Sav was a good sleeper, an hour at least – you could stick pins in his forehead and he wouldn't wake up. He wouldn't be left alone really if there was an emergency; Mumm-Ra would be in the house. If Gran arrived, Jem could say she'd had to nip to the chemist for some more of something. That seemed sensible. She was always being told how sensible she was. It was annoying, especially as she was only just not eleven anymore. Today she wanted to see what was going on, like everyone else. The baby and the dog would probably even be on the news.

She did Sav a nappy in the bathroom and put Vaseline on his bum, shielding herself from a wee spout with a towel. He loved weeing when his nappy was off. Men loved weeing up against trees and in the underpass and in the park and they started very young. Jem was getting good at nappies. She could do them much faster than Mumm-Ra. It was mostly Gran and Jem that looked after Sav though so there was plenty of practice. Jem put the dirty cloth in the dirties basket, which was getting full. The nappy man came on Sunday nights and Wednesday nights, but Sav had gone through quite a few with a bout of something runny. The nappy man was a stupid old-fashioned person and it was embarrassing to have to open the front door to him, hand over a smelly bundle, and get a clean bundle back. Even though a lot of people were using disposables, he was still in business. Mumm-Ra said disposables were expensive and it was better to keep a person in work. She snapped at Jem when Jem asked who made the disposable ones then? Why do you have to be so contrary, madam? Contrary.

Jem hated the nappy man, partly because what kind of man wanted to wash poo for a living, partly because he had a van that said *Mr Nippy Nappy Man* on the side like a giveaway, but mostly because he had a funny eye. He had an eye with a golden gash in it, like a gold disease of some kind. The eye didn't move about much. His other eye was blue and normal. She sometimes wondered who had the worst job, the nappy man or Mumm-Ra. Mumm-Ra, probably.

Jem carried Sav back to the bedroom, got his library books out then sat on the beanbag to read to him. He squirmed into position in her lap and she fended off his pointy elbows and heels. Moon, he said. Sav was heavy and half her size already, who knew how because he didn't eat anything. Moon, he said. What about Ant and Bee? Jem asked. She hated *Goodnight Moon*. The colours were horrible. The little rabbity creature in pyjamas was horrible. The strange page near the end was extremely horrible. It gave her the same feeling as jumping down off somewhere high, or looking up at the sky for too long. She tried to slip the book under the beanbag but Sav spotted the cover. He scrambled to get it, took hold of Jem's hand and made her hold it. Moon! OK, OK, mister.

She let him turn the pages as she read. Sav pointed items out in a slow, serious way as she said the words – toy house, mouse, comb, brush, bowlful of mush, quiet old lady whispering hush. She tried to flip ahead to the end of the book, past the weirdest bit, but Sav wedged his podgy fist between the pages so she couldn't avoid seeing

Goodnight nobody

Sav turned and looked up at her, frowning. He didn't understand, but neither did Jem. Who was nobody? Was nobody actually somebody, a person there but not-there in the room? Could the rabbity creature see nobody from its bed? That was like a ghost story for babies, which was very wrong. And if it was a joke she didn't get it, because it wasn't funny. It was exactly the opposite of funny, and opposites always created problems. The opposite of married. The opposite of love. The opposite of alive. She nudged her brother and blew on the back of his head. He smelled of milk and potato and nappy detergent. Come on, she said, turn the page, Sav. Sav turned the page. Jem read to the end of the book, then tried to lift him up and put him in his cot, but he grabbed her T-shirt and barnacled to her. Moooon!

After three more *Goodnight Moon*s he let her put him down. He shuffled about, stuck his legs through the bars of the cot, kicked, yawned, then rolled onto his stomach and went to sleep immediately, as if someone had unplugged him. Under the sticky orange, his hair was thick and dark. He looked nice when he slept, Jem thought, loose and soft, not like the Lego-hurling, crusty-nosed monster he normally was. Sav always wanted things doing for him and showing to him. Being the one who knew more was hard work; she often didn't like it. Maybe he dreamt of Yugoslavia when he slept.

Maybe he dreamt of his dad, though he'd never met him, and his dad might be dead. Could you dream of a place or a person you'd never known? Gran said Sav would have a lot of questions when he was older.

Jem put a blanket over him. She thought about going outside. She thought about the little baby, lying in the basket, and pictured its neck like a chewed-on dog's bone. Mumm-Ra's bedroom door was shut. Silence and darkness behind it, like the Black Pyramid. Jem went downstairs and turned on the TV, but there was only motor racing on, flimsy cars on a noisy, skidding track. She got her book out and sat at the kitchen table.

The street was quiet by the time Gran arrived, just a few people coming back from the city with carrier bags and their hoods up. Drizzle had started. The police van wasn't there anymore. The dog had probably been taken away. Mumm-Ra had already gone back to work and wouldn't be home until morning. When she'd left the house she was pig-eyed and late and on the point of being extremely cross because she couldn't find her keys. She'd forgotten her box of sandwiches on the kitchen counter – she ate sandwiches for dinner at work as if it were lunchtime. Things always felt topsy-turvy when Mumm-Ra was on night shifts.

Jem walked down the cut between houses, to the football field, and along the backs of the yards. There were empty crisp packets skittering about, a flat, dented football. The back gate of the man's house was battered and blistered. There was police tape across it – the only sign anything terrible had happened there. Jem could smell dinners cooking, crispy pancakes and meat and gravy. She could smell rain on the bricks. People were inside waiting for the evening news. The baby might have a name and it would be announced. Could you name a baby after it was dead? Or maybe they'd use an initial, like the little girl who had gone missing from the park last year. Baby R. Rebecca, Jem had guessed, or Rachel. Gran was making cauliflower cheese for their dinner, which Jem didn't like because the cauliflower was usually soggy and the sauce always had flour-lumps and hardly any cheese. Gran would ask her about boys at school, which was embarrassing. Anyone look like that lovely Lion-y character? Jem never corrected her.

Mortuary. Decapitated. When you thought things, like words, it was because there was a voice inside your head that said the thoughts. Jem hadn't realized that before. The voice wasn't exactly your voice, but it wasn't anyone else's.

There was no point hanging around outside by herself. She walked back along the yard walls. If she were friends with Deborah she could go and knock on her door and ask if anything else had happened. Deborah's door was white plastic. In the upstairs window – Deborah's bedroom, maybe – was an A-ha poster. She could imagine Deborah's face when the door opened, a big how-dare-you sneer. The rules would definitely be back by now. Off on your own, duck-fuck? Where's your Yoogi brother?

Jem looked at her watch, which was blue leather and quite nice, a birthday present from Martin last year. He'd forgotten her actual birthday and had given the watch a week late. Overcompensation, Mumm-Ra said. It was quarter past five. She was supposed to be back by six. Sometimes Martin came to see her on Saturday afternoons for tea but not every Saturday. Jem didn't have Martin's surname, Steele, which he complained about, but it was too late now. He didn't have any other children – none that he admitted to, Gran said. Steele would have been a good surname. Martin was the only other person Jem knew who liked *Thundercats*. He watched a lot of television, even cartoons; he said cartoons were ace and philosophical. *Thundercats* hasn't caught on yet, he told her once. They're all too different from each other, too distinct. But they have the same emblems, she'd said, and they all follow the code of Thundera. Not the same as a uniform, he'd said.

Jem walked back down the cut. On the street a bus passed by with *Out of Service* on the front. It never made sense when buses drove along out of service – they were still going somewhere and could drop people off and be useful. They were doing exactly what they said they weren't. She walked down the road towards the Saracen's Head, which smelled of beer and vinegar. A dog was tied up outside – a border collie. Its tongue was long and pink and tipped up at the end like a spoon with spit in. She looked at its mouth for a while until she felt a bit sick, not with a bug, but a sort of strange worried sickness.

She turned and walked home. She opened the door and went through the front room into the kitchen, where Sav was playing with pots and pans on the floor, and Gran was having a cigarette at the table and reading the newspaper. Clouds of cauliflower steam billowed from the cooker. Hi, love, said Gran. Jem picked up the box of Mumm-Ra's sandwiches. I've got to go and drop these off, she said. Her face felt like it was glowing pink but she'd said it, matter of fact, like it was on a list of things to definitely do. Oh, said Gran, that's nice, you've certainly got a spur in your heel. Do you know the way? Yes, said Jem, get off at Ashton Road. Gran nodded. OK. I'll keep a plate warm for you.

Jem waited a moment. Sav held his arms up for a carry, but she ignored him. Her face felt very hot now. Her armpits felt tingly. She waited for it to all fall through, for there to be a telling off, though Gran never told her off. Her heart was clapping, quite fast, as if it was applauding the brave performance. Mostly you didn't feel your heart, only after sprinting or when you were afraid. Gran turned the page of the newspaper. Bye then, Jem said. Bye, love, said Gran.

Sav wailed as she walked away. Jem got to the front door and opened it. She went outside. She walked down the street, past Deborah's house, past the dog and the pub. When you were sensible, you were trusted to do things. You could look after your little brother alone in the house. You were allowed to find the hospital on the bus, even though you didn't know exactly where you were going. She had 50p in her pocket. She didn't have her coat. Gran hadn't even made her take her coat.

A bus was coming in the right direction. She half ran to the stop. The sandwiches bumped about in the margarine tub. She might have to stick them back together again for Mumm-Ra. She waved, and the bus stopped. Jem got on. The driver had smeary jam-jar glasses and didn't seem to care who she was. I have to get off at the hospital, she told him, Ashton Road. He nodded. She waited for him to say how much the fare was, but all he said was, Sit down then, Cuddles. The bus moved and jerked her forward as she walked down the aisle. There were no passengers except for a couple of women in brown cashier smocks and a man in a hat who was asleep against the window. Jem sat near the front, though the back seat was empty and she never got to sit on the back seat going to school, like Deborah did. She sat with the sandwich box balanced carefully on her knees. She could see a purple wrapper in one corner through the plastic. A biscuit. A fruit Club, probably. They were Mumm-Ra's favourite.

It took ten minutes to get to the hospital. She kept looking at her watch, the big hand ticking round. The town was dark silver in the rain, like pencil lead. The bus went past the prison and the castle, up the one-way system. People were already going into the pubs. A few umbrellas bobbed along. The streetlights were on.

She'd been to the hospital once before, not to visit Mumm-Ra, Mumm-Ra wasn't working there then, but to have a bean-shaped growth removed from her chest. She'd lain on a table covered with white paper and they'd given her a stinging injection to numb the patch and she hadn't felt them cut. She'd looked at the ceiling the whole time and a nurse had held her hand. She'd had eight proper stitches afterwards, with thin black string because they couldn't use paper ones. She'd pulled the stitches out early because they were itchy and the hole had gaped open. There was a silky white scar on her chest now, a bit like a spider's sac, which her T-shirt covered. They'd done tests on the bean but it was harmless.

Jem got off the bus at Ashton Road. The driver didn't tell her where it was but she could see the hospital looming. She walked across the crossing. Ambulances were parked in a bay outside and as she walked towards the main doors one of them turned on its siren and whirling light and blared off. In front of the main doors, under the dripping porch, was a huge pregnant woman and an old man in a wheelchair with a metal stand next to him. A clear bag hung from the stand with a tube snaking down. It was rude to stare but Jem couldn't help it. The man didn't even look like a person. He was slumped over in the wheelchair. His bare shins poked out under his gown and his feet were purple and lumpy, like bruised vegetables. The gown was the same as the one Jem had worn, white with little blue diamonds.

Some patients died here, some died on the way here, and some were dead when they arrived. It didn't matter to Mumm-Ra, though maybe the ones who were dead or died coming were harder. They would have bad injuries, like motorbike smashes, and the baby attacked by the dog. They might be in pieces. Decapitated. Jem tried to stop looking at the man in the wheelchair. He would be going to the mortuary soon. The rain was very light again now; she could just about feel it on her nose, as if the rain was only thinking about what it was supposed to do. Most people thought working with dead people was a man's job, according to Gran. When the job had been advertised Mumm-Ra had interviewed and got it. She had the right disposition, Gran said. She's always been like that, your mother.

The Royal Infirmary was old, several storeys high, with an even taller tower, but also new bits built on the sides. Hospitals had to keep getting bigger, because more and more people needed them and there were new cancers all the time. It was hard to picture Mumm-Ra anywhere, touching cold hands and faces, talking to relatives with orange baby food staining her back. She would probably have new scrubs on. Jem could picture her at home, on the sofa, tired, her head leaning on her hand, eyes closed, or staring at something on the other side of the room that wasn't really there. Mumm-Ra's staring always made Jem nervous.

The signpost of departments outside the main doors didn't list the mortuary. Jem could ask at reception. She could even leave the sandwiches at reception and someone might take them to the mortuary and Jem could go home. Probably they wouldn't even let her go to the mortuary, you might have to be eighteen, like for pubs and some fairground rides. She looked at her watch again. If a bus came in a few minutes, she could be back home by six o'clock, to Gran's cauliflower cheese, to Sav throwing water out of the bath and screaming when his hair was shampooed, to watching telly until later than normal because it was Saturday.

The woman on reception didn't seem concerned when Jem asked where the mortuary was. She pointed to a door on the other side of the building, described the way through the hospital, and then let Jem go, just like Gran had. Follow the blue line, the receptionist said, until you get to pathology, then turn right. Pathology sounded like a joke that actually was funny, though Jem felt too wobbly to laugh. She walked down a corridor, past several wards. A dinner trolley was going round. There were lots of old lopsided ladies. There was lots of coughing. She remembered the hospital smell from when she'd had the bean off; it wasn't as bad as everyone said. It was sort of aniseedy. A couple of doctors walked past and looked at her. One smiled. He had on a paper hat and a kind of paper apron, like a man who worked at a meat counter. Maybe he thought she was a patient. Maybe he knew Mumm-Ra, Jem looked more like Mumm-Ra than Sav did. People said they had the same eyes, hazel, which wasn't brown, and wasn't green, but was both mixed up. Gran said quite often that Mumm-Ra should marry a doctor. Not my type, Mumm-Ra always said. Exactly, Caroline, exactly my point.

Jem followed the blue line. She didn't get lost. The Royal Infirmary wasn't very big really. She went down some steps, then up some steps, out a back door and past a few prefab huts until she got to a small plain building with a sign on the door. Mortuary. Jem stood outside. The doors opened and a woman came out and she also smiled at Jem as she walked past. The woman didn't look like she'd been crying. Maybe she was a secretary. The door swung closed. Mortuary. The building looked like a building where nothing important happened, like one of the humanities huts at school. She'd expected something frightening, tall, sooty, with ivy or broken windows, like a haunted house. This wasn't that.

Something caught her eye and she looked to the side. Next to the mortuary was a small car park with yellow lines painted on the concrete, which meant cars couldn't park there. Parked on the yellow lines was a long black car, with an oblong window: a hearse. It was right there. She could see in. You were supposed to see in. On the back shelf was a coffin. It was made of dark, very shiny wood. Someone had polished and polished the wood. There were brass screws and handles and there was a smooth brass plaque with nothing engraved on it. No name. No birthday. Nothing. There were no flowers around it, like when hearses went to the church and made other cars drive slowly.

Another ambulance siren wailed in the distance. Jem stood outside the mortuary.

There was a rush around her, a feeling like jumping off a wall, like before throwing up. She wanted to sit down. She wanted to run back along the blue line, all the way to the bus stop, all the way home. It wasn't raining at all now. The rain had stopped. It was almost evening, almost six o'clock, the end of the day. But Mumm-Ra was working. She was inside the building, with the bodies of people who didn't exist anymore. She might be holding the little dead baby, carefully, combing its hair, buckling a tiny shoe strap, doing some makeup to blush its cheeks, or she might be holding the hand of a relative, the man who owned the dog, the man's girlfriend who people had said didn't care. Her mother would never die, because she couldn't, though all of this, all this, would be taking its toll.

Jem stood outside the door and held the box of sandwiches. She wanted Mumm-Ra to see her through the window and come out and put a hand on Jem's head, even if she was cross, and Jem couldn't really tell her why she had come here. Not the sandwiches. She wasn't even sure what the sandwiches were. Cheese? Fish paste? Egg? She didn't know. She lifted the lid and smelled inside the box. Egg.

· One in Four ·

My darling Christine,

I can't call you that, I know, but I still love you and the children very much. I'm sorry you're reading this, sorry I wasn't stronger. I know I let you all down. You were never supposed to be involved, but how could you not be involved. It's all such a mess. Don't let Nicky and Dominic believe everything negative. I can't bear the thought of them hating me. I can still see Dominic's face the last time I tried to talk to him. I won't try again. I wake up at night terrified that they've caught it. Or that you have. We're in the second wave now, I'm sure of it. Stay safe. It'll be you at risk, Chrissy, your immune system is stronger, a liability – you know that already, you've heard me say it a million times. If you feel sick, with anything, don't go to the doctor, don't go anywhere public and crowded. I wish I could make you promise me. And don't ask for the anti-viral. People are queuing up for it but it doesn't work, it'll just make you think it's worked. I never told you but that was my idea, my brand name – Vedi-flu. After Vediovis, the god of healing. What it does to the ego, creating such a thing. We all become gods. You found it dull, my work, didn't you? All that boring theory. 'Cytokine storm sounds about as interesting as it gets,' you once said. Look at the storm now. Tents outside the hospitals, chaos, people drowning in their own fluid. It looks so different outside the lab. I used to think the virus was beautiful under the microscope. A beautiful planet, with so many reaching arms. It's such a clever little thing, Chrissy, it uses us to kill us. We're the perfect weapon.

I want the kids to know – I didn't bury the trials. I didn't lie. Maybe I didn't shout loud enough about ineffectiveness, but I followed protocol, I raised it at boardroom – you must remember me doing that? I said, slow down, it isn't ready, when Cochrane get the full data the company's reputation will be damaged. They didn't listen. Listening isn't profitable. No one was ever going to stop it, certainly not me. They're a government agency, Chrissy, at least the CIC is funded by Eli-Meyer. I've seen emails. My computer's gone now, so I can't prove it. And Sharon Blake doesn't answer my calls, she's on a book tour is what they told me. The newspapers aren't interested anymore. Yesterday's whistleblower, what a fucking joke. They just want the epidemiologists, the A & E stories, the end-of-the-world stuff. At least someone's getting rich as well as Meyer. That picture of the little boy asleep on a bench at Paddington, everyone walking past him – except he isn't asleep, is he. I keep seeing it everywhere, can't get away from it. They did that to him. I know, I know, this is more of the same, and you've heard enough to last you a lifetime. I just need you to understand.

Anyway, bottom line. It is my fault. I helped make a drug that makes people feel well enough to go out and infect others. They're saying that one in four will die – a quarter of the population. A hundred years after Spanish flu and we're no safer. Maybe I should just wait, I might get a lucky draw, might end up in the morgue myself. But I've had enough, Chrissy, they're rinsing me. The phone calls don't stop. I moved four times last month but they always find me. They're clever bastards, they know how to open you up, how to climb into your brain. Always at night, when everything seems so hopeless. Or it's just after the school run, when it could be you phoning, because something's happened. And the other things. They moved my car last week. Just to the other side of the road, but they moved it. And the deliveries – pornography mostly, but then letters from the bank, accounts I don't even have, all overdrawn, and, you won't believe this, Mum's funeral bill! £2,863.80 for a wool coffin, roses and freesias – she loves freesias, how did they know? How could they have asked her that when she can't even remember her own name? The undertaker doesn't exist – I phoned them. I got sent a new number plate last week – H6N1. The police don't care. Everyone thinks I'm mad. Some kind of ranting madman. They won't even let me on the library computers anymore because they say I make too much fuss, I disturb people. I know they sent you that letter and the photos and I'm sorry. I should have told you myself, but I was afraid you'd leave. And now you have left. Maybe I do deserve it all. I wish it would stop. Why don't they stop now – I'm finished, everything's finished.

I just keep thinking of our old garden in Stokenchurch. We always had such good light in the trees in the evenings, didn't we? And that swing the kids loved. God, I miss it. I'm not going there – I wouldn't do that to you, even though I know you've left. The woods at Merryhill. It's quiet, not many people, I don't know another way. I've been afraid for months and months, I can't really remember anything else, but I'm not afraid now. Funny how you begin to feel better once you know what to do, once you get out from under it. I've been so tired, Chrissy, and sick in my heart. You don't realize how small and weak you are until you're shown how big everything else is. The truth is, we're all so desperate to carry on, but we're nothing really, just specs on the glass. I've spent my whole life trying to find a cure, and here it is, all of a sudden.

J.

· Evie ·

She arrived home after work, sat at the kitchen table and took a large chocolate bar out of her bag. She said nothing, not even hello. She split the foil, broke it apart, and proceeded to eat the entire thing, square after square; a look of almost sexual concentration on her face.

Had a bad day? he asked.

She smiled faintly.

Not like you to go for the junk. Did you miss lunch?

She shook her head. Her jaw moved, slow and bovine, working the substance against her palate. She was looking but not seeing him. There was something endogenous about the gaze, something private, as if his presence in the room was irrelevant. She ate the entire bar, methodically, piece after piece, while he put the kettle on and began dinner. He heated a pre-made lasagna in the oven, opened a bag of salad and dumped it into a bowl. She ate only a little of the meal.

I guess the snack ruined your appetite.

Her eyes flickered up from the plate.

Yes. I don't know why I had the whole thing. Only,

I'd been thinking about eating some for days. Then I had to.

She didn't apologize for the wasted food. Usually she would; she was the type who apologized over any minor or innocuous discourtesy. He wondered if she was angry with him, whether a passive campaign was playing out, though he could think of nothing he'd done wrong.

Over the next week she began to eat chocolate regularly. She would snap off portions while watching television or between chores. In her car smeary wrappers were strewn on the floor. She'd never had a sweet tooth before, had never ordered dessert in restaurants. She'd always kept her figure because of it. Now, she seemed addicted. And not just to chocolate, but anything sugary: pastries, puddings, fizzy drinks. She would leave her steak or pasta half finished, leave the table, and come back with something glazed that she'd evidently bought in a bakery between her office and the house.

God, I just can't seem to stop with this stuff, she said one night.

It was true. She went with a predatory look to the cupboards. She wasn't thinking, just acting on impulse. She was drinking more too. Wine with dinner every night, a few extra glasses at the weekend; becoming gently hedonistic. They'd been for a meal at Richard's and she'd finished a bottle of Cabernet by herself, as well as the lemon torte he'd served.

Hey, hey, Richard had said, taking her hand and helping her up from the couch, after she'd slumped on the first attempt to rise. Nice to see you letting your hair down, Evie.

How gallant, she'd said, a mock-belle voice. Then, whispering, I know you want this.

She'd leaned up and kissed him. A kiss not on the cheek, but on the mouth: a deliberately erotic move that implied nothing less than seduction, as if her husband, sitting next to her on the couch, did not exist. At first, Richard had been too dazed to respond. This was a glimmer from a long-desired, alternate world, where his best friend's wife was available to him. After a moment he roused himself, took hold of her wrists, and looked over to the couch, as if to say, *here, hadn't you better intervene.* Evie was staring at Richard's mouth, her lips parted, her lashes lowered. Together they'd helped her into her coat and into the car. Once the seatbelt was buckled and the door shut, Richard had turned to him.

That was a bit unusual. Is she all right?

Evie's head was drooping to one side; she was asleep, or passing out.

I don't bloody know. She's all over the place lately. She's fine, I think.

What do you mean all over the place?

Just acting up. For attention, maybe. I don't know. She's fine. Sorry, Rich.

You're sure?

Yeah. Yeah, just had a few too many.

On the drive home the incident had preoccupied him. The look of desire, the unboundaried gesture. It wasn't that she hadn't looked at him that way in the past – nights when they were at their best, their least inhibited, when the act was intentional rather than habitual. But to see her looking at another man. It'd shocked him, and Richard too, clearly. But it had also been exhilarating. Something had flared inside him. Possessiveness, naturally – she was his wife – but there was another sensation too. Pride. Or worth. He didn't quite know. She suited the attitude; perhaps most women did.

He glanced down at her legs as he drove; the skirt riding untidily on her thighs, the flesh pale in the glow of the streetlights. Her arms were cast out either side of the seat – he'd already moved one away from the gear stick – in a pose that looked supplicatory, almost religious. She roused minimally when they arrived home, walking into the house and upstairs like a somnambulist, lying on the bed fully clothed. He'd run a hand up her thigh, but by then she was unconscious.

She had a hangover the next day and he caught her having a shot of whisky in the kitchen. Her makeup was smudged round her eyes. The silk robe was loosely belted, with one breast partially exposed.

For God's sake, Evie. Didn't you have enough last night?

Hair of the dog, she said.

You're acting like a student. That's going to make you feel far worse.

Let's see.

She tossed the spirit back.

Boom!

She set about cooking pancakes for breakfast, which she coated with syrup, rolled up and ate with her fingers. He sat opposite at the table, refusing the plate of glistening batter, choosing instead a frugal bowl of muesli. He was annoyed with her; he didn't know why. She was acting a little irresponsibly, a little outlandishly – but so what? He'd always wanted her to be more cattish, hadn't he, like the girls at university he remembered who had tattoos before it was popular, who wore tiny shorts, took pills every weekend and danced on podiums in the union. And the thing with Richard; he knew there was nothing to it. Richard was too restrained, too safe, almost neuter; he was always ill with something and in need of sympathy; he'd never been a genuine threat. It occurred to him she might be pregnant, and hormonal. Though surely she would know, by now, and the drinking was very inappropriate. Evie wasn't like that.

She was washing up at the sink, her rings set aside in the small ceramic dish, her bottom shaking as she scrubbed, hips a fraction fuller under the gown, though not unattractively so. He asked her.

Pregnant, she blurted, half turning. I don't think there's much risk of that, do you?

Offended by the overt reference to their irregularity – usually they both avoided the topic with practised denier's skill – he stood and made to leave the room.

Wait, she said. Maybe, well, what do you think?

About what?

About getting pregnant.

Are you serious?

She dropped the scrubbing brush into the basin of soapy water and wiped her hands on the silk robe. The material darkened and stuck to her skin.

Actually, no. But I would like a fuck.

He was stunned. It was not the look of the previous night, but it wasn't the usual furtive pass that one or other of them made, when it had been building a while, and before an argument occurred.

Would you? she asked.

She unbelted and moved the robe away from her midriff. The pubic hair was in a neat brown strip. She'd waxed. He looked at her. He was angry now, at the guilelessness, the domestic crisis she seemed intent on creating. Why was she being so bald? It made no sense. The atmosphere around her was unsettling, like irregular weather. He was jealous, and impressed by the approach, by her making a stranger of him almost. All the times he had wondered, imagined getting his cock out, stroking himself in front of her and saying, *come here and suck this*, how she would have responded. He'd never done it. Neither had she, though he'd fantasized often enough about her masturbating in front of him, kneeling, her legs apart, or on all fours. The answer was yes. But he did not speak or move. She was looking at him, her face unblushed, not ashamed, not desperate. There was only so long such a precarious, risky moment could go on, before it spoiled. He was hard. He knew what he should do. Hostility got the better of him.

What are you trying to prove, Evie? What?

She shrugged, a one-shouldered shrug, the definition of nonchalance. She left the robe open and sat down. She lifted one foot up onto the chair seat. He could see more of her cunt, the folds and dark seam. He felt hot and uncomfortable. He should be kissing her, feeling her breasts, doing what she'd asked him to. But this exchange; there was too much and too little intimacy at once. He disliked her casualness, the request as banal as to go and buy milk. He was locked in. It was absurd.

I mean, what are you doing? What are you *doing*?

Asking you to go to bed with me.

I mean, you're being just bizarre. You haven't even showered. You're a mess. You're ruining yourself with junk food. You're having whisky at ten a.m. and saying mad things to me in the kitchen. And then last night. What was that?

I just want a fuck, Alex. That's all. If you aren't up for it, fine. Maybe later.

She leaned across the table and wiped up a viscous smear from its surface, put her finger in her mouth. She was not upset. The transaction hadn't worked, and that was that. Part of him felt ashamed for attacking her, for the impotence of his mood. But she'd walked carelessly across the tripwires of their relationship, as though through a field of mines, as if immune. And her response to the rejection was ludicrous, like a child's or an autistic's. He turned and left the room.

He had never really loved his wife, not with acute, debilitating passion, the kind that was lionized and sung about. He had become fonder of her over the years, and more attached. She did nice things for him – making him sandwiches to take to work, buying replacement toothbrushes when the bristles on the current one began to splay. Other men found her attractive; colleagues often commented on his good fortune, and Richard had had a thing about her for years. Richard always remembered her birthday, procuring thoughtful and not inexpensive gifts, taking her side in quarrels, though there weren't many. Objectively, she was a catch, but he'd never felt dizzyingly emotional about her. He'd never tortured himself with the idea that she might leave, or stop loving him, that she was irreplaceable.

The first thing he'd really liked about her was her name. Evie. Like a forties starlet. He'd had a spell of dating women with interesting names, in and after university: Lola, Oriana, Kiki, Simone. They were never as interesting or free-spirited as their names suggested. He'd expected vivacity and petulance, oblique intelligence, someone who would perhaps be difficult to manage, but fascinating and worth any trouble, inspiring something torrid in him, lust leaning towards deviancy; someone who would cancel out the desire to upgrade, someone with whom he could experiment and live interestingly.

Good crazy, rather than bad crazy, that's what you want, Richard had said. A fantasy woman. But it's bullshit, Alex. You keep getting them to fall for you, then cutting a swathe. It's ridiculous.

He had gone through a number of them, telling himself he was on a romantic quest. They were all trying for unique jobs – dance therapists, writers. Often they wore clothes that suggested originality, unusualness: red chiffon shirts with showing-through bras, men's brogues, even rebellious vintage fur tippets. They were confident at first, sometimes conceited. He encouraged them to audition for the part, which gave them licence. Once the novelty of the sex wore off, once they failed to be uniquely talented, he struggled to make a connection. Under the faux exoticism, they wanted husbands, money, big town houses. Or they really were fucked up. By six weeks he was usually disappointed or bored. Or things had exploded.

The last – Simone, the children's musician – had proved disastrous. After her various antics and tantrums, he'd tried to phase her out. She'd turned up at his door, incensed, had made an aggressive pass, and they'd gone to bed. The following day, after he'd explained his position, she accused him of trying to get her pregnant, dragging him to the doctor's for the morning-after pill, and making him watch her 'miscarry'.

By the time he met Evie he'd given up on the idea of exceptionality. They met at Richard's Christmas party. She was lively; the men in the room were crowded around her. He introduced himself to those in the group he didn't know, weighed her. She was copper-haired and trim, bright-eyed, but not stunning. She didn't have a bone structure that suggested lifelong beauty. They danced. She moved well, neat but suggestively.

Her eyes were big and pretty. Richard kept bringing a bottle over and offering to top them up, trying to join the conversation. Why not, he'd thought.

Their dates were pleasant. Evie was pleasant. She smiled a lot and dressed well. He liked that other men were attracted to her. There was no sulking or ego maintenance. In a way it was a welcome compromise after the extreme terrain he had attempted. But she wasn't stupid. She could tell he was withholding, he was making no declarations; there was no obvious lovers' trajectory. It came up one night in a restaurant and he told her he wasn't sure exactly how he felt about her. He didn't feel anything tremendously, for anyone. There was an argument, unshouted, but definitely an argument.

I don't move you in any great way then? she asked. What am I, wallpaper? Just there in the room?

No. Listen it doesn't affect the relationship, he said. We're having a good time.

Are you mad? Of course it does. I want more than that. Who wouldn't?

She'd stood up, unhurriedly, gathered her coat, and left. It was a superior, graceful exit. He'd tried to phone her but she ignored the messages. She started dating someone else soon after; he heard about it from Richard, who'd stayed in touch with her. This bothered him; no, it piqued him. He couldn't stop thinking about her and the new lover. He wondered if his emotions had been lagging, or had been masked. He'd lasted a month and then he was on her doorstep, saying he couldn't be without her, asking her to marry him. He almost convinced himself. By the end of the evening they'd had sex several times – it was as close to anything meaningful as he'd ever felt – and they were engaged. It all played out. They married. They bought a house. It was fine.

He remained angry for the rest of the day. He washed the car. He fixed the puncture on his bike. He stayed outside as much as he could. Evie lazed about the house eating sweets, listening to the radio and flicking through magazines. When he spied on her through the window she didn't seem to be unhappy or brooding. She made cups of tea at intervals. She painted her nails. Whatever was going on, she was clearly capable of holding out. He was angry, but he was interested too.

In the afternoon it began to drizzle, the wind got up and a proper shower arrived, darkening the tarmac driveway. He became sick of the oily stone-floor smell of the garage and the glum bare bulb overhead, so he went inside. He made a quick circuit of the lower floor. Evie was not there. He could hear faint noises from the bedroom upstairs. Halfway up he paused and listened. There was a rhythmic sound, alternating between a purr and a wail – female. After a moment it became clear what it was. He moved across the landing and opened the bedroom door. She was lying on the bed, on her side, naked, her hand between her legs. The laptop was at the end of the bed. He couldn't see the screen but he could hear the slapping of flesh, the groaning.

What's going on?

She kept her eyes on the screen.

I found this site. Her voice was low, distracted. I like this one best.

A burning sensation rose up his neck. His chest was flurrying. He waited a moment, then went over to the bed. On the screen a man was fucking a woman from behind. His fingers were gripping her buttocks, indenting her flesh. There were tremors in her body every time he thrust. The camera angle showed the penis moving in and out, glistening. The image was mesmerizing. And embarrassing. Not because he hadn't seen anything like it before – it was all too familiar – but because his wife was in the room, watching.

I like this bit, she said.

The man on the screen pulled out of the woman. She presented herself, wider. Her genitals were depilated, the flesh dark purple. The man knelt, put his face between her legs and began to tongue the crease. Evie rolled on her back, held her head up so she could still see the screen.

Take your clothes off, she said.

He was aching painfully. He had forgotten everything else. The automatic took over. He undid his jeans, pulled them down, pulled his unbuttoned shirt over his head. He wrestled out of his briefs. Evie knelt up. They did not kiss. She crouched and took him into her mouth. He looked down at her back, past it to the screen, where the man was pushing apart the cheeks of the woman and re-entering, higher. After a few moments Evie took her mouth away, moved back and turned round. He was rough with her. He wanted to slap her. He didn't understand any of it, but it didn't matter, everything had become reasonless. She was moaning. The other woman was moaning. A visceral harmonic. On the screen the man was pulling the woman's hair so hard that she was rearing upwards, her back bent at an extraordinary angle. He knew he would come soon. Between sounds, Evie was saying things that made no sense, some kind of rapturous, incanted language. Then:

Do that if you want. Do that to me.

He put his hand into Evie's hair, made a fist and pulled. He was breathing so hard he felt crazed. He pulled out and repositioned. He made a series of small movements. The muscle clenched and then relaxed. He worked himself in, began to move. The knowledge of its happening was exquisite. It was too much. He felt himself climax, noise blared from his mouth, and he slumped against her.

They lay for a while, the film ended, and then he gently moved away. Evie reached over and scrolled through the contents page of the site. He looked at the mess on the sheets, pleased, mystified.

It happened every night, and in the mornings, before work. They did not always watch pornography, though often she wanted to. It began with her instigating, but then he realized there was ongoing permission. For anything. They tried different ways. They videoed themselves on the digital camera. He saw a man like him performing oral sex, licking slowly, then frantically; he watched his wife handling herself with no inhibition. He didn't recognize the woman staring straight into the lens. She did not want foreplay or romance. She wanted candid and carnal exchange. While it happened she spoke mad words, unconsciousness.

It's inside the daylight. Making each other wet. It's all the way in. In.

There was something almost shamanic about it. She looked as if she was trancing, her pupils blown, as if the act was commanded, unstoppable. The expression of confused pleasure and fear and drive was spectacular. Her breasts were heavier and swung beneath her, or juddered when she was on her back. What excited him most was when she talked about other people joining them, another man.

Oh, God, both of you inside me. I'll do anything, anything. I'll do anything.

I'll watch him fucking your pussy. I want to see you ride him, make him come all over you.

The rules were gone. It was easy to say these things; easy to undo himself. They'd suddenly found each other, through irrepression, means he did not quite understand. Her age, hormones, a revival of some lost appetite, the arrival of a new one; it didn't matter, he didn't care.

Towards the end of the third week he noticed she was damaged and bleeding and asked if she was sore. It didn't matter, she said. She wanted to carry on feeling this way; her body finally knew what it was meant for. She made him, again. There was more blood, an alarming streak up her rump and on the sheets. He didn't want to stop but something was wrong. A person did not become so extreme, so mercurial, without cause. While she took a bath he searched through her bag, for what he wasn't sure, drugs perhaps, prescription or otherwise. Lipsticks, tissues, chocolate wrappers, a discreet white vibrator, which he hadn't known she owned. There was a letter from her work. She'd been cautioned for inappropriate behaviour in the office. When she came out of the bathroom he asked about it.

You dropped this. It says you've been saying things to other members of staff. Is that true, Evie?

I don't know what the bloody problem is, she said, throwing the wet towel onto the bed. They're just so boring, so glass. They don't get it.

Don't get what?

What you have to do. You've got to make it happen whenever you can.

Make what happen?

I can't explain it speaking, Alex. Come and lie down.

He lay next to her on the bed. She put his hand between her legs. He took hold of her wrist.

No, come on, he said, softly. Try to explain, Evie. What's going on?

Don't be angry.

Then she began to cry. Short rapid bursts, without tears. She sounded almost like a baby. A lump rose in his throat. What was coming? He put his arms round her and held her. The flesh on her stomach was plump and warm. She'd become a baroque version of herself, a decadent. The crying did not last long. She did not wind down, but suddenly sat up, the distress forgotten.

I tried to get Karl to sleep with me. Then I asked Toby. You weren't there. I wanted you to be, but you were at work.

What?

Will you help me? I have to know how it feels. I can't stop thinking about it.

About what?

Her face was hovering in front of him; open, beguiling, altered.

You and me and someone else.

He had known she was going to say it; the scenario had featured too strongly, too mutually in their role-play to be insignificant. But he knew too that there was a line, over which, if they passed, there was no coming back. The dynamic would always be changed; they would be beyond themselves.

Please. I want to. It would be amazing. Like a sun in us. It tastes like, I can taste it burning.

She put her hand to her mouth with a sharp intake of breath, as if scalded.

You say these things, Evie. They don't make any sense.

I have to do it. We only live. We only live, Alex. Such a tiny thing. I know how to feel. This is the truth. Do you believe me?

She moved close to him again. She put her hands on his face. Her eyes. Electrical green, and gold, powering the irises.

You choose. You choose who. You bring him. I'll do anything you want.

In her gaze was something retrograde, pure, unconstructed desire. She was more beautiful than he had seen.

Why is it the truth?

I don't know. It's a gift.

He convinced Richard to come out for a few drinks midweek. Richard asked where Evie was.

Busy. Joining us later, was all he could say.

Which sounded chary; they never deliberately excluded her. He was drinking quickly, nervously. He knew it had to be spontaneous, natural, Richard would never agree otherwise. He looked at his friend across the table in the pub. He couldn't imagine it. They'd been roommates at university but he'd never really heard any explicit details about girlfriends from Richard, or witnessed moments of intimacy. Perhaps going with a stranger would have been better, but that seemed reckless. He bought them both another pint and then a whisky.

Whoa there, slow down, Richard said. I'm going to get hammered. I am hammered.

Yeah, sorry. Just wanted to cut loose a bit. I tell you what, let's leave these. Come back to ours and we'll have a nightcap with Evie?

I thought she was coming here?

No. Come on.

They left the pub and walked back towards the

house. They walked without coats. The air was warm. The world seemed looser.

You and Evie are OK though?

Really great. Revolutionary!

Oh. Good. God, I haven't felt this drunk in a while. Thought you were getting me loaded so you could confess something bad. Like an affair. I'd have killed you.

No, he said. Just fancied a fun night. We're not that old yet.

True.

The lights were on downstairs when they arrived, but Evie was not around. He called up, saying Richard was here for a drink. He was sure he sounded like a bad actor, overdoing lines, like the hammy utilitarian films Evie had been watching. He didn't know how she would play it. She'd been so direct, so layerless lately, it was possible she'd scare Richard by moving too quickly. Whatever was in her now used no subtlety. They'd talked about what might happen, what kind of lover Richard might be, how receptive, but the truth was there was no predicting; shock, disgust, willingness. They were gambling.

She came downstairs wearing a nightgown, her hair wet, as if just washed. She smiled at them both. The room seemed charged. Precognition. It was going to work.

Richard, she said. She kissed him on both cheeks

and then on the mouth, playfully, laughing.

Richard's face was flushed, from the beer, the walk, from the pleasure of seeing Evie. She sat down on the couch and began to talk in the way she did now, synaptically, brilliant and baffling. He could see Richard listening, trying to follow, enjoying her. He left them and went into the kitchen and took a bottle from the wine rack. He uncorked it, poured and drank a glass, then brought the glasses and bottle into the lounge.

Let's have a really good night, he said, too loudly.

They drank the bottle and opened another. It was fun, it was ridiculous, they played stupid games, Evie flirted with them both, he and Richard conspired. She leant against their legs, against their chests. She dropped the shoulder of her gown and showed Richard a small new tattoo. It began soon after. It began almost unnoticeably, like a season, a regime. It was unreal and then it became serious. The protests – there were only a few from Richard, we should stop now, come on guys, this is madness – were overridden. Evie reassured him. He reassured him. Once she was unveiled, once Richard saw her, allowed her to take his hand and place it, once he began to believe there was nothing prohibitive, even in himself, that there was just love, everything accelerated. The laughter died away. They were clumsy and aroused. Richard was surprisingly confident. There were no condoms; they knew each other. It went on for a few hours, each of them took turns. She always invited the other back in. He wanted to watch from the chair; he watched her being touched, grasped, opened, watched her responding. He began to understand: jealousy was only desire; it was wanting to do what he could see was being done to his wife. They went upstairs and fell asleep. Once he woke to see Richard going down on Evie. It was amazing, more sensual than anything he'd imagined. He reached over. He felt ill and elated. They were still drunk but there was clarity. They slept, woke. He remembered a moment, or he was in a moment, when Evie was bent over in front of him; he was moving behind her, Richard was kneeling in front and she had him in her mouth. The two of them were joined by Evie's body. They were facing each other. It would be all right afterwards.

He slept again. The next time he woke it was because Richard was calling his name and hitting him on the shoulder. White dawn light. His head was splitting, his mouth tasted evil, bitter.

Alex!

He looked over. Evie was lying on her front on the bed, her legs apart, jerking. She was making long, low sounds, bellows, almost cowlike. There was a smell like offal.

She just started going, Richard said. I don't know

why. I was on top of her. Help me turn her over.

He moved to Richard's side and the two of them rolled her. There was foam across her face and in her hair, the smell of bile and alcohol. He tried to keep her head still but her neck muscles were snapping up and down. Her eyes were white in her skull, her jaw clamped, the spit oozing out.

What the fuck. Evie! Evie! Call an ambulance. Should we drive her?

No. I'll call.

Richard leapt up and went downstairs. The convulsions in his wife were so strong it felt as if her spine would break. Then they began to ease. Richard came back in. He had trousers on. His face was ghastly.

They're coming. Christ, what's the matter with her. What kind of fucking depraved game is this?

A junior doctor asked him questions in the family room of A & E. About the fit. About whether she'd had headaches lately, or vomiting, vision or memory loss – he did not think so, he said. And her behaviour: had there been any changes? In what way? Had he been concerned?

They had ruled out stroke, toxicity. She was sent for a CT scan. The junior was evasive, professional, but the scan was not a good sign, he knew. Richard had followed the ambulance in a taxi, had sat with him on the hard plastic chairs while they'd sedated her and run tests, had fetched coffee. But they did not talk. *I didn't know*, he wanted to say, though no blame had been directed. The silence was blame. The repeated enquiries about his wife's state that he'd been fielding from his friend for the last few weeks were blame. There was no point in them both waiting. He promised to call Richard with any news.

A consultant came and found him in the family room. The scan had shown an area of the brain that appeared abnormal, in the prefrontal cortex. They didn't know yet what it meant. But the appearance was suspicious.

Do you mean a tumour?

We need to investigate.

The same questions were asked, more focused, the chronology of her cravings, her confusion, her promiscuity, the man nodding at the answers, as if already confirming a diagnosis. When they let him see Evie she was asleep. He found her hand under the sheet. She didn't wake. In the light of the small overhead lamp she looked normal, unextraordinary.

Everything after was the penalty for some unknown crime. The MRI pictures. The whitened shape. She was lucky and unlucky, they said. The mass, though probably benign, was big. He couldn't remember the word after the meeting and had to look it up. *Meningioma*. It was not in the important tissues – he did not really understand what could be unimportant inside the brain – but pressure was swelling the surrounding area, interfering with her functions, her cognition, her self. Over the next few weeks she had more fits. The second broke her wrist. She choked on her vomit and infected a lung.

She was given drugs to control the seizures. They began radiotherapy. The operation was scheduled. He could barely stand to think about the procedure – the position was difficult, she was ineligible for Gamma Knife or endonasal surgery, she needed a craniotomy. He looked online. The pictures were medieval. Rent-open heads. Pinned-back scalp. Lilac membranes and manes, so horribly wet and delicate. In one video a surgeon described the sound of cracking the skull, *like opening a can of Coke*. They would try to keep the incisions behind her hairline, but plastics might be required. The risks were extensive; leaks, aneurysms, coma.

She still wanted sex. She still strung wrong words together, talked like a charismatic, her mind slipped and was instinctive. But she knew what it was now. She was self-conscious, and fought for rationality; she contained it. When they were in the act she would claw away and start to howl and they would stop.

This isn't me, she'd say. I don't know if it's me.

She was not afraid. She knew she would live.

Recovery would be tough, unpredictable, relearning; she might not be or feel exactly like the same person, ever again, but she would live. He didn't know if it was her, believing, or the lambency, the mania of the illness. It was an illness now. It had a name.

They had told Richard soon after the final diagnosis, convincing him to come over for dinner, saying that the meeting was vital, not a set-up. He had wept. Evie had looked at him, expressionless, and left the room.

Jesus Christ, Alex. Why her?

She'll be OK, he said. She's tough.

Richard shook his head.

You fool. Do you not understand? What don't you understand?

They sat without speaking, sipping their drinks, until the evening dissolved.

Richard phoned the morning of the surgery but did not come to the hospital. He phoned regularly afterwards, but did not visit. The decision to withdraw was obvious, even gracious. It was difficult, but he didn't mind. He was glad that it wasn't completely broken off. On the phone they talked about things of no consequence. Work, weather, the past. They never talked about that night, though he thought of it, often, more often than he should.

· Acknowledgements ·

Versions of these stories have appeared in the following: The *Guardian*, the *New Statesman*, BBC Radio 4, *Reader I Married Him*, *Royal Academy Magazine*, and *Vice*.

'Mrs Fox' won the BBC National Short Story Prize, 2013.

'Evie' was shortlisted for the Sunday Times EFG Private Bank Short Story Award, 2013.

Thanks to the following people for reading, editing and commenting on versions of these stories, and for artistic, medical and general feedback: Lee Brackstone, Kate Nintzel, Peter Hobbs, Jon McGregor, Damon Galgut, Clare Conville, Jane Kotapish, Dr Richard Thwaites, Tom Gatti, Dr Ben Irvine, Rebecca Watts, Dr James Garvey, Dr Frances Brooke and Lucy Ashton-Geering.